MUCH ADO ABOUT MURDER

NEVERMORE BOOKSHOP MYSTERIES, BOOK 7

STEFFANIE HOLMES

BACCHANALIA HOUSE

Cover design: Amanda Rose

ISBN: 978-1-99-116044-7

✿ Created with Vellum

MUCH ADO ABOUT MURDER

All's fair in love and murder.

The Shakespeare Festival has come to the village, and all of Argleton has gone bard-crazy. Mina's excited about Nevermore being the festival's official bookstore, but a rival bookshop opens up across the green and completely cramps her style.

When the bookshop's owner is found clobbered to death by his own First Folio, Mina and Quoth are determined to stick their nose (and beak) in to solve the case. But with a real Shakespearean fairy running around the village and Morrie determined to curse the performance, Mina and her men already have their hands full.

With help from a troublesome Puck – and absolutely *no help* from Mina's mother's latest scheme – will they solve the crime and save the festival, or is it the final curtain call for Nevermore Bookshop?

The Nevermore Bookshop Mysteries are what you get when all

your book boyfriends come to life. Join a brooding antihero, a master criminal, a cheeky raven, and a heroine with a big heart (and an even bigger book collection) in this fun and steamy reverse harem paranormal mystery series by *USA Today* bestselling author Steffanie Holmes.

Grab a free copy *Cabinet of Curiosities* – a Steffanie Holmes compendium of short stories and bonus scenes, including one from Quoth's POV – when you sign up for updates with the Steffanie Holmes newsletter.

JOIN THE NEWSLETTER FOR UPDATES

*W*ant a free bonus scene from Quoth's point of view and Heathcliff's shop rules? Grab a free copy of *Cabinet of Curiosities* – a Steffanie Holmes compendium of short stories and bonus scenes – when you sign up for updates with the Steffanie Holmes newsletter.

www.steffanieholmes.com/newsletter

Every week in my newsletter I talk about the true-life hauntings, strange happenings, crumbling ruins, and creepy facts that inspire my stories. You'll also get newsletter-exclusive bonus scenes and updates. I love to talk to my readers, so come join us for some spooky fun :)

*To all the book boyfriends
who keep me up at night.*

"Out, out, brief candle!

Life's but a walking shadow,

A poor player that struts and frets his hour upon the stage, and then is heard no more:

It is a tale told by an idiot, full of sound and fury, signifying nothing."

– Shakespeare, *Macbeth*.

CHAPTER ONE

"Jesters," Morrie grinned. "Definitely jesters."

"And fairies." I smiled as we stepped onto the town green, heading toward the brightly-lit Rose & Wimple. "And a bloody dagger. And do you think we could make him wear a ruffle?"

"Aarf!" Oscar added his two cents.

Heathcliff rolled his eyes. "My kingdom for a horse to trample me to death right now."

"C'mon, Sultan of Sourpuss." Morrie leaned in to pinch Heathcliff's bum. "Let Mina ruffle you up and later, I'll do that thing you like with the spatula and the geranium—"

"Lalalalala, I can't hear you." Quoth covered his ears with his hands.

"I was only kidding about the ruffle, but we've got to bard Nevermore up a bit. The annual Argleton Shakespeare Festival starts next week, and the town will be full of people visiting the bookshop. We need to get into the spirit, or we'll miss out on potential business." I dropped to my knees in the grass in front of Heathcliff and clasped my hands in front of me. "Please? Just a small display of books and a jester's hat in the window—"

Heathcliff glowered. "To quote Hamlet, Act III, Scene III, Line 87, 'No.'"

"Arf, arf!" Oscar admonished Heathcliff.

"We're joint owners," I pointed out. "That means you can't stamp your foot and make the rules. If I want to bard-up the shop, then it's happening. So get on board, or off with your head…"

I trailed off as I realized Heathcliff was no longer listening. He stopped dead in his tracks in the middle of the town green, his mouth hanging open in shock.

"Ow." Quoth crashed into him from behind. "Why the traffic jam? Let's just get to the pub so I don't have to hear about any more geranium abuses."

"Heathcliff?" I waved a hand in front of his eyes. The greatest gothic antihero in all of literature didn't even blink. His haunting gaze was focused on something in the distance, something I couldn't see.

"It's finally happened," Morrie moaned dramatically, placing his hand against Heathcliff's forehead. "All that internalized rage has loosened his brain cells. He's lost his noodles. The Stilton cheese has slipped off his cracker. The wheel is spinning, but the hamster is dead—"

"What the fuck is that?" Heathcliff growled at the darkness.

"What the fuck is what?" Morrie peered all around, but didn't seem to notice whatever had Heathcliff so flummoxed.

"*That.*" Heathcliff jabbed a thick finger across the green. "What the fuck is *that?*"

I turned to look, but of course that did sweet bugger all because I couldn't see across the green. Quoth squeezed my hand. "The old flower shop has new owners," he said. "It looks as though they're opening a bookshop."

A bookshop?

My first thought was excitement. I loved bookshops. I have ever since I was a kid and Mum would leave me to read in a dark corner at Nevermore for hours while she went about her various schemes. But then I remembered that I was now co-owner of Argleton's *one and only* bookshop, which already struggled with paying our bills now that so many people shopped online on The-Store-That-Shall-Not-Be-Named. Having a competitor around the corner, with a prime location right on the village green, could spell disaster for Nevermore.

I swallowed back my concern. "Let's take a look before we judge." I grabbed Heathcliff's arm and directed Oscar to walk us to the new shop. Sun Tzu said you needed to know your enemy, and that was exactly what we'd do.

The lights were off inside the shop, so I couldn't see a thing through the window. Morrie cupped his hands over the glass, peering into the darkened depths. "It's an antiquarian bookshop. I see shelves of dusty old volumes in velvet cradles with price tags in the *thousands*. This joker isn't going to last a week in a village where people think *To Kill A Mockingbird* is a how-to guide for rural pest control—"

"Why, hello there."

Morrie jumped. Oscar barked at a man who poked his head from the doorway. The streetlamp fell across his face, illuminating a viciously hooked nose, thin lips, and chubby cheekbones that looked like they'd been pinched by one too many grandmothers. A pair of piercing dark eyes regarded us with amusement that brought to mind the terrifying, shadowed face of Count Dracula. That wasn't at all fair as a comparison but then, *he* was the man lurking about in a gloomy shop.

"Arf!" Oscar greeted the man.

"Who's this boy?" The man stooped, holding his hand out to pat Oscar.

"That's Oscar. He's my guide dog," I said, and the man retreated his hand. Obviously, he knew not to pat a guide dog while he was working, which warmed me to him. "Oscar was just saying hello. We didn't mean to disturb you. I'm Mina Wilde, and this is Heathcliff Earnshaw, James Moriarty, and…er, Allan Poe. We were curious about the new shop, and the lights were off so we didn't think anyone was inside—"

"Don't worry, I quite understand," the man chuckled. "You're here to scope out the competition. I did exactly the same thing – I was in your store last week, Ms. Wilde. I know who you all are, and when I saw you heading my way through the window of my upstairs flat, I had to rush down and greet you."

"Wait, are you saying that you—"

"I must say, you have a curious store policy when it comes to customer service. I asked about the first edition of *Ulysses* you have advertised on your website, and Mr. Heathcliff here told me that I should go next door to the bakery and eat a whole cheesecake if I wanted something dense. And on my way out the door, your store raven defecated on my shoulder, ruining a perfectly good Gieves & Hawkes jacket."

Gieves and Hawkes. That's the Savile Row tailor who holds royal warrants to dress the Queen and the Prince of Wales. This guy is either rich or full of his own self-importance. Or both.

"I remember you now," Heathcliff snarled. "You're the smarmy git who was too big for his britches to apologize to Grimalkin for standing on her tail. As far as I'm concerned, fair's fair. And I stand by my earlier statement. I was trying to save you from a literary headache – reading *Ulysses* is like unprotected sex; it's fun at first, but after four weeks you're praying for a period."

Great. I was hoping to establish a friendly relationship with our new competition, and we'd got off to a *smashing* start.

"I take it Grimalkin is the delightful black temptress who shoved a decapitated rat through my mail slot last night. Please extend to her my greatest apologies for any injury caused. I can be *awfully* clumsy." The man's voice oozed fake sincerity. "My name is Jasper Rasmussen. Mina, may I shake your hand?"

I held out my hand, and he took it and shook, squeezing my fingers a little too hard.

I take back my earlier assessment. This guy is a complete prat. I shall tell Grimalkin to leave him a welcome present on his pillow.

"Welcome to Argleton, Mr. Rasmussen," I said with all the fake sincerity I could muster. "We're excited to have a fellow bookseller in the village. When will your shop be open? We'll be sure to tell our customers to check out your stock."

"The grand opening will be tomorrow," he said with pomposity. He disappeared inside and returned a moment later with a flier, which he handed to Morrie.

"Rasmussen Books: Rare, Antiquarian, and Fine Literature," Morrie read aloud. "Specializing in appraisals, inscriptions, and authentication services for the discerning collector."

"See?" Rasmussen clapped his hands together. "Your little shop has nothing to fear from me. After perusing Nevermore's selection of *popular books*, I'm certain our clientele will not overlap."

He said *popular books* like it was a curse word, which set my teeth on edge. Oscar growled, tugging on his harness. Oscar was an excellent judge of character.

"It says here that you're the official bookstore of the Argleton Shakespeare Festival," Morrie said, a note of accusation creeping into his voice. "That's not possible. *We* are the official festival bookstore. It was set up months ago. We have all the stock ready to go."

"That may be so, but I have something special that will delight the festival attendees," Mr. Rasmussen beamed. "I'm displaying a genuine Shakespeare First Folio."

I gasped. A First Folio was a collection of 36 of Shakespeare's plays, published in folio format in 1623, seven years after his death. (I'd been brushing up on my Bard facts). The First Folio was considered one of the most influential books in the whole history of reading, and was the definitive scholarly source for around 20 of Shakespeare's plays. Approximately 750 First Folios were printed, and 235 were known to still exist – mainly in private collections. One recently sold at Christie's for nearly £10 million.

And Rasmussen was going to have one on display in Argleton during the Shakespeare Festival.

How could Nevermore Bookshop ever compete?

CHAPTER TWO

"He's a damned and luxurious mountain goat," Heathcliff huffed as he slammed down his empty glass and reached for his second pint. "A sodden-witted lord who hast no more brain than I have in my elbows. His wit's as thick as a Tewkesbury mustard."

"These are excellent barbs," Morrie beamed. "Really top-notch stuff."

"Quoth got me a book on Shakespearean insults," Heathcliff thumped his chest. "I've extended my repertoire."

I turned to Quoth – who sat beside me in the booth – and placed my hand over his. Ever since he'd fallen under the spell of Dracula and unknowingly helped the count choose his final victims, he'd been performing these little kindnesses for us. He cleaned the flat until it shone, he left us little gifts and surprised us with home-cooked meals and loving touches and poetic words. Quoth was already a complete sweetheart – he put everyone else before himself – but this new frenzy of affection carried an air of desperation, as if he had some great cosmic list he had to tick off before he could receive absolution for his sins.

I hated it. I hated that he suffered when he'd already been

through so much. I hated that he blamed himself, and that nothing I said or did could make him see that *Dracula* was the guilty one, not him.

I wanted to take Quoth aside right now and talk to him about all of it, but with Jasper Rasmussen and his First Folio in the village, we needed to strategize.

"It sucks." I rested my head in my hands. "No matter what we do, we're never going to top a genuine First Folio."

"You can put me in as many ruffles as you want," Heathcliff said gruffly. Under the table, he rubbed the edge of his foot against mine.

"It won't help. People are going to flock to Rasmussen's store and forget all about us. We'll lose all our word-of-mouth. And he doesn't even *like* this village. You heard what he said about our *popular books*. He thinks everyone in Argleton is an illiterate yokel."

"*We* think everyone is an illiterate yokel," Heathcliff pointed out. "Just before, Morrie was saying that people in this village think *To Kill A Mockingbird* is—"

"I know what he said! But that was just a joke, a friendly jest about people we care about. We're allowed to joke because we've been part of this village for years. But he doesn't get to waltz in here like he's God's gift to books and lord it over us. I know healthy competition is part of business, but we already struggle, and I hate that we're not the only bookstore in the village anymore. And Heathcliff's right – Rasmussen is a sodden-witted goat."

"He hath more hair than wit," Heathcliff added, a cruel smile breaking out on his face. "And more faults than hairs, and more wealth than faults."

"Exactly. And *why* is he telling people he's the official bookstore of the festival?"

"He must be mistaken," Quoth said. "Mrs. Ellis would never sell you down the river like that."

"The birdie's right. It's an error, and we'll get it straightened out right now." Morrie waved at someone over my shoulder. "Mrs. Ellis, over here!"

A moment later, a familiar carpetbag brushed my leg and a warm, wrinkly hand landed on my shoulder. "Mina, boys, it's so good to see you again."

My old English teacher slid into the chair next to Quoth and pinched my drink straight from my fingers. She had a deliciously filthy mind (and mouth) that constantly landed her in hot water, but she was our number one source for village gossip. She'd recently revealed that she knew all along that Heathcliff, Morrie, and Quoth were characters in a story, and even helped us vanquish Dracula and hide all the supernatural goings-on from the rest of the village. And she was the head of the Shakespeare Festival committee for the tenth year running, so she was just the person we needed to straighten this out.

"Good evening, Mrs. Ellis. You're looking particularly lovely tonight," Morrie said in his most charming voice. "Would you like to join us for dinner?"

"Oh, you're a sly fox, Mr. Moriarty," Mrs. Ellis simpered as she sipped my drink. "As much as I'd love to accept your offer, I have too many preparations for the festival to attend to. I'm only here because I need to check that Richard has prepared all the food we need for opening night."

"Excellent news. We were wondering if you noticed the new shop in the village, Rasmussen's Books…"

"Oh, yes." Mrs. Ellis shifted uncomfortably. "I'm not sure we'll have much call for his fancy books in the village, but I guess there are always people with more money than sense. He's a remarkably strange fellow, if you ask me."

"We thought so, too. The thing is, he seemed to think he was the official bookshop of the Shakespeare Festival. But that can't be right—"

"Oh, dearie me." Mrs. Ellis finished my drink in one gulp. "I suppose I need to talk to you all about it."

I didn't like the tone in her voice. Oscar stirred at my feet, sensing a shift in the air.

"Talk to us about what, Mrs. Ellis?"

She reached across and swiped Heathcliff's drink from his hand. "You see, it's just that Mr. Rasmussen has very generously offered to display his First Folio and other items in his rare Shakespearean collection as part of the festival. And obviously that's quite a draw for our little village. It will bring people from miles around. But only under the condition that he was able to run the festival bookstore."

"But...but *we're* running the festival bookstore," I spluttered. "We've been prepping for months."

"He's an antiquarian bookseller," Heathcliff growled. "He knows nothing about arranging stock for an event like this."

"He says he'll make an exception for the festival," Mrs. Ellis said. "He has contacts with all the best book people in London, and he came with impeccable credentials, so the committee isn't worried. I'm so sorry, Mina. I *did* fight for you, but the committee had pound-signs in their eyes when he pulled out that First Folio. I meant to tell you sooner, but I've been run off my feet with festival stuff. I told your mother at the last Spirit Seekers Society meeting to break the news to you, but I'm guessing it slipped her mind."

For once, I couldn't be angry at Mum for this disaster. She was so utterly besotted with her new boyfriend, Handy Andy (the village's not-so-handy handyman), that she'd been even more scatterbrained than usual. I loved seeing her so happy, especially since being in love meant she wasn't around at Nevermore every day trying to foist her latest harebrained get-rich-quick scheme on our unsuspecting customers.

I sighed. "It's fine, Mrs. Ellis. Thank you for letting us know."

Under the table, Oscar barked. I reached down to calm him.

That's not like Oscar. Guide dogs were trained not to do that while they were working unless there was an immediate danger.

Morrie turned around in his seat. "Good spotting, Oscar. If it isn't the devil himself. Mr. Rasmussen has just walked in. And who's that he's with?"

I could see four figures taking their seats at a table near the bar. Mr. Rasmussen's hooked nose stood out a mile away.

Mrs. Ellis leaned over the table, a conspiratorial glint in her eyes. She may not have been able to give us that festival slot, but she always had the village gossip. "On his left is his only daughter, Shelley. She lives in the caravan park next to the estate. Mr. Rasmussen moved to Argleton to be closer to her and her son, Max. And on the right is Mr. Lawrence Delacroix, who is Mr. Rasmussen's apprentice. He scours the country looking for treasures in old estates and junk shops while Mr. Rasmussen manages the shop. Mr. Rasmussen is training him in the delicate art of the book trade."

"What delicate art?" Heathcliff growled. "You order books. Books show up. You sell the books. You order more books. You stare into the empty void of your bank account until your soul shrivels up and dies. That's the book trade."

Ms. Ellis ignored him, which was the best way to deal with Heathcliff when he was in this mood. "I'd love to keep chatting, but I see Richard escaping out the back—yoohoo, Dicky." She lurched from her chair and chased the fleeing tavern owner across the room. "We need to talk about those mini Yorkshire puds—"

I stared in melancholy silence at my empty glass. Wordlessly, Quoth slid his drink across the table in front of me. I accepted it even though I knew I shouldn't get in the habit of using booze to absorb emotional blows. *One Heathcliff in our family is enough.*

"I'm sorry, Mina." Quoth leaned against me, touching his cheek to mine in that intimate way of his that melted my heart. "I

17

know you were excited about the festival. At least we still have our backstage work to look forward to."

"This could be a good thing." Heathcliff shoved aside his empty glass and reached for the third he'd ordered as Morrie got up to head to the bar. "At least the shop will be blissfully free of ruffles and thees and thous."

And income, I thought but didn't say.

All those books, hundreds and hundreds of playbooks and biographies and picture books about *A Midsummer Night's Dream*, and even a series of Shakespeare plays told in text speak, all those hours I spent with Zenzile Monroe at the Argleton Shakespeare museum, coming up with the perfect selection of scholarly texts and pop culture, all that money we outlaid on signage for our table and a portable point-of-sale system that I could operate...

"You'll feel better once you drink your sorrows." Morrie slid back into his seat, four drinks clutched in his long fingers. He pushed another G&T under my nose. "That's the British way."

"And at least we're still doing the sets and costume design," Quoth added, his voice rising with hope.

Morrie snorted. "If Rasmussen hasn't taken that over, as well."

"Why does Rasmussen even care about this festival? He does know that Shakespeare isn't high-brow entertainment for elitist wankers?" I growled as I slammed down my empty glass. "Shakespeare wrote for the people in the yard. Anything can seem arty and important if it's presented in a certain way, but Shakespeare is supposed to be melodramatic pop culture. That's why his work has endured. People like Rasmussen make me so angry when they make out that classic literature is somehow this deep art form that can only be understood by a select few, when really they're just plays filled with gore and special effects and fart jokes."

"*There's* the Mina I know and love." Heathcliff slammed his glass down on the table. His hand touched my knee and slid up my thigh, his fingers brushing between my legs.

"Preach it, gorgeous." Morrie pumped his fist in the air.

I was on a roll now. "If the bard were alive today, he'd think this festival was hilarious. It would be as if people in the future were dissecting the *Fast and the Furious* franchise in scholarly debate. Shakespeare would laugh all the way to the bank, and I don't—"

"Rasmussen!" A booming voice echoed across the room. "Where's my book?"

My rant died on my lips. The entire pub fell silent. We turned toward the voice. Quoth, who was excellent at quietly describing things that were going on to me, whispered, "There's an enormous American fellow striding across the pub toward Rasmussen's table. He's wearing a white suit with an American flag tie and a cowboy hat, and a face like someone just told him the pub's gone vegan."

I covered my mouth to hide my snort. Quoth's descriptions were usually spot-on.

"I know him. That's Hiram Abernathy," Morrie whispered. "He's a Texas oil baron and an avid collector of old, elitist, wanky books."

"He sounds angry," I whispered back, sipping my drink. "How do you know him?"

"*Please.*" Morrie rolled his eyes. "He's a *Texas oil baron.* Suffice it to say that over the years, he's occasionally been in need of my less-than-legal services."

I decided it was better not to inquire further. Besides, some sort of drama involving Mr. Rasmussen was playing out in front of us, and I was here for it.

"Ah, Mr. Abernathy." Mr. Rasmussen stood and gestured to an empty chair at his table. "Come and sit with me. I'd like you to meet my daughter, Shelley, and my associate, Mr. Delacroix. We'd be delighted if you—"

"Cut the corndogs, Rasmussen. I'm fixin' to bring my First Folio back to America with me, and I want to know why you agreed to my perfectly reasonable offer and then upped and left me in the lurch without so much as a howdy-do."

"Mr. Abernathy, as Mr. Delacroix has explained to you, we never officially accepted your offer. We have our duties as guardians of the literary history of this country to ensure the First Folio is on display to the public for the duration of the Shakespeare Festival. After that, I'm willing to entertain all offers, including yours."

Mr. Abernathy pounded the table with his fist so hard the mushy peas rolled off the edge. "Dagnabbit, man, I need that folio *today*. My wife Petunia is obsessed with this Shakesword fellow—"

"—Shakespeare—" Mr. Rasmussen corrected with a sad sigh.

"—and she's on a plane heading this way *right now*, and if I don't have it in time for her birthday tomorrow, she'll whip me like a redheaded stepchild."

At the back of the bar, a woman shouted. "It's a travesty to sell such an important historical document to this man. He already owns *seven* First Folios. He doesn't need another. But the Argleton Shakespeare Museum would be grateful for such a vital donation. We would digitize the text so everyone could access the wonder that is Shakespeare's work. If Mr. Rasmussen really cared about the literary history of this country, he'd do the right thing and donate the First Folio to the museum."

"I know who that is," I grinned. "That's Zenzile Monroe, Zen for short, curator of the Argleton Shakespeare Museum. She helped me choose the books for the festival."

"We have a Shakespeare museum?" Heathcliff sounded shocked.

"Oh yes, it's that cottage behind the post office." I must've visited that museum twenty times as a kid on various school trips, as it was the one taste of culture within walking distance. It was a single room containing some cardboard displays about Elizabethan theater and the one connection Argleton had to the

Bard – a letter from the magistrate warning Shakespeare's father that he needed to pay his debts in the county or risk the displeasure of the Crown. Given how stabby and beheady Queen Elizabeth got when she was pissed, I imagined Shakespeare's old man paid up quick.

"Father, that's an excellent idea. You should donate the Folio." Shelley Rasmussen's voice rose. "Zen is the village's Shakespearean expert and a dear friend. She would take good care of it, and I know that's important to you. Do the right thing, for once, and give her the book."

"It wouldn't even need to be a donation," Zen said. "The museum has a fund for new exhibits. We've saved almost twenty thousand pounds, enough to put in an offer on the book."

"That's right." I had a coin jar on the counter a few months ago to help raise funds for the museum, until Heathcliff said children might mistake the coins for candy, and made me get rid of it.

Hiram Abernathy snorted. "Darlin', I offered this man fifteen million for the book. You don't stand a snowball's chance in hell."

"Please, Daddy?" Shelley tugged his sleeve. "Don't sell the book to this man and have him lock it away. Max loves visiting that museum, and I think it would be wonderful for him to be able to tell people about his grandfather's gift to the village—"

"Ssssh," Mr. Rasmussen told her sharply. "This is business, my dear. You don't understand anything about it."

"I understand that I'll inherit your business one day and that I'll run it very differently." She slammed her fist into the table. As if on cue, her son started to wail. "You have to take me seriously at some point. I hoped you opened the shop in the village because you were finally going to teach me your trade, but instead, you bring along this apprentice I've never met. Do you really trust me so little?"

"It's not a matter of trust, my dear. Lawrence and I have been working together for four years now. He has built relationships with my buyers, like Mr. Abernathy here, that I can't simply walk away from—"

"Waaaaaaaaah."

"It's a travesty," Zen shouted over the screaming baby. "You and your kind deprive scholars of precious historical documents that could tell us so much about life during Shakespeare's day. It's not fair—"

"All's fair in love and war," Hiram Abernathy shot back at her. "Isn't that what your beloved bard said?"

"Shakespeare never said that. See?" The woman's voice grew shrill, incensed. "He doesn't even appreciate the Bard's work. He just wants to own things. He wants to lock the First Folio behind glass where no historian can study it and pat himself on the back for being a man of culture and refinement, when really he's a dirty rotten thief trying to steal away something that should belong to everyone—"

"Lady, you are all hat and no cattle." Hiram tipped his hat. "Why I oughta—"

"Ladies and gentlemen, *please*." Lawrence Delacroix stood up. He was a willowy man, as tall as Rasmussen was wide, with a kind, open face. "There's no reason to fight. We're trying to do what's best for everyone here. We're exhibiting the book precisely so that anyone who wants to can see it. No one is a bigger fan of the Bard than I am – I was a Shakespearean actor in college, you know. I won an award for my Titus Andronicus. But you must understand that we are a business, not a museum, and we must recoup our costs. When the festival is over, we'll be delighted to sell the First Folio…to the highest bidder."

"That'll be me, then." Hiram thumped his chest.

"Isn't there a saying where you come from – don't count your chickens before they've hatched," Zenzile sniped back. "We might have a trick up our sleeves yet."

"Well, aren't you precious? You think you have a shot? My wife *will* have this book, even if I have to ruffle a few feathers or wring a few necks." Hiram wagged his finger at Rasmussen. "I warn you, Rasmussen, don't dig up more snakes than you can kill."

Hiram's boots clacked loudly on the floorboards as he stormed out.

"I don't speak Texan," I said to the guys as the pub hummed to life again around us, "but that sounded like a threat."

CHAPTER THREE

"Foul temptress, thou hast stuck me," Puck moaned.

"Sorry." I shoved the pin through the hem of his pantaloons and reached for another.

"Curses. Thou hast done it again."

"If you didn't squirm so much, I might be able to hem your pants without you losing a pint of blood."

"Fine. I shall be as a statue."

Puck stuck his tongue out at me as he struck a pose with one leg out to the side and his arms raised above his head like a ballet dancer. He froze, completely refusing to move no matter how much I tried to shove his arms down so I could fit his costume.

"You'll look lopsided, and you have only yourself to blame," I muttered as I pinned his hem at an absurd angle.

Quoth, who was watching the proceedings from a nearby table, where he was painting a plywood tree, disappeared behind a Scottish castle drawbridge. A moment later, a raven emerged and flew straight at Puck's face, wings flapping.

"Crooooak!" Quoth pecked at Puck's cheeks until the fairy had no choice but to fend him off.

"All right, all right, call off your bird of prey." Puck cowered from Quoth's onslaught. "I shall behave, for now."

We were backstage at the New New Globe theater, a recreation of the traditional Elizabethan theater where Shakespeare's plays were first performed. Only, instead of being made from wood and thatch like the original Globe theater, the New New Globe was built of very modern steel scaffolding and plonked smack-bang in the middle of Argleton Comprehensive's rugby pitch for the duration of the festival. Three plays – *Macbeth, A Midsummer Night's Dream*, and *Romeo and Juliet* – were being put on with actors drawn from the village. Once the festival was over, the theater would go on tour around the country, "popping up" in villages and towns, bringing Shakespeare to the people and giving everyone a chance to experience life in front of and behind the curtain. It was such a fun idea.

The whole thing was the brainwave of local entrepreneur Miles Shackleton, who wanted to take our annual community theater festival and make it bigger and brighter and better. He proved himself to be a man of genius when he roped Mrs. Ellis into heading up the festival committee. Mrs. Ellis asked me to be responsible for costumes for the *entire festival*, and even though I was hopelessly busy with the shop and the three men in my life and wrangling my mother and her insanity, the fashion designer in me couldn't possibly refuse.

My eyesight was now gone to the extent that I often couldn't see the color of a garment unless I was standing in extremely bright light. But that didn't mean I'd lost my love for fashion. Quite the contrary – I'd discovered an appreciation for texture, shape, and drapery that I never had before. I now loved clothing with bling – beads and sequins and anything shiny because it caught the light and sparkled, and my eyes could pick up on that, and it lit up happy thoughts in my brain.

I was *born* to make costumes for the stage.

I loved stepping into the crowded costume room behind the

Lord's Rooms, running my hands over the beautiful fabrics and trims, and working with the theater team to design clothing that would look stunning from every angle and still allow the actors to move freely. For the first time since I left New York City, I was enjoying fashion again without thinking about what I was missing out on.

And it didn't hurt that Quoth was working in the same room, designing the sets and props for the three plays and genuinely being all cute and Quoth-like. If only he'd stop hating himself for the Dracula thing, and Mr. Rasmussen would decide running the festival bookshop was too much hassle and give it back to us, life would be perfect—

SLAM.

I jumped as the door banged against the wall, half expecting Dracula himself to fly through. But we vanquished that old bloodsucker a few months back, and after Heathcliff fixed the shop's plumbing, no other fictional characters would randomly appear. *So who—*

"Excellent news." Morrie's voice boomed as he strode toward me, picking me up under the shoulders and spinning me around. "Macbeth is here for his costume fitting."

Oliver – the village baker in the shop on the corner of Butcher Street – was supposed to play Macbeth, but he tripped over a bag of flour and broke his ankle, and so Mrs. Ellis had called upon Morrie as his understudy to step into the role. From the way Morrie had been going on about it, it wouldn't surprise me if he'd had something to do with Oliver's "accident" – he was, after all, the Napoleon of Crime. I dropped my pincushion and gestured to the rack of garments. "Right this way, noble king."

"Please, call me Macbeth—"

Behind me, Puck gasped. "No, no, no, no." He jumped up and down. "You cannot say that word in here."

"What word?" Morrie sounded confused. "Macbeth?"

STEFFANIE HOLMES

"Argh!" Puck spun in wild circles, slapping his cheeks and crying out, "Fair thoughts and happy hours attend on you."

Morrie frowned at Puck. "What's he doing? He does this funny little dance every time I say 'Macbeth'."

Puck wailed as he spun faster, spouting off more lines from Shakespeare.

"It's a theatrical superstition," I explained. "Apparently, when Shakespeare wrote the play, he used a real witches' spell for the 'spotted snakes with double tongues' speech, and the coven he nicked it from cursed the play with bad luck if its title is spoken within the walls of the theater. Actors have literally died on stage during fake sword fights or by sets falling on them. Puck's performing the cleansing ritual to ward off the witch's curse—"

Morrie leaned in close and whispered against my ear in that dark, mischievous voice of his, "I know, sweet Mina. I know all about the curse. I just wanted to see the fairy dance."

*A*ll afternoon, actors came in at their allotted times for their costume fittings. Quoth helped me wrangle them into their costumes and hang up their outfits on the racks with tags for their names and the scene changes.

"Who's next?" I called to the blurry gaggle of people waiting by the makeup tables.

"That would be me," a familiar female voice said as she stepped up onto the box. "Nice to see you again, Mina. It's Zenzile Monroe. I'm playing Lady Macbeth."

"Ah, you're my beautiful and conniving wife." Morrie took her hand and kissed it.

"Mr. Moriarty, I look forward to sharing the stage with you." She stepped up onto the block I was using for fittings and spoke. "'You spirits that tend on mortal thoughts, unsex me here. And fill me from the crown to the toe top-full of direst cruelty.' You

28

know, I really do wish a Shakespearean spirit would fill me with cruelty, so I could do to that Rasmussen character what he deserves."

Puck appeared behind her, his finger raised and a cheeky grin on his face. Morrie elbowed him in the ribs so hard that he toppled over, the wind knocked out of him. Good. The last thing we needed was Puck gifting Zen with Shakespearean vengeance. There were enough prop swords around that she could do some serious damage.

By Isis, if we can get through this festival without any murders, I'd appreciate it.

"We overheard your argument in the pub last night," I said as I started pinning Zen's skirt. "I'm sorry Mr. Rasmussen cares more about profit than scholarship. If you must know, we're not exactly thrilled with the way the guy does business, either."

"Yes, I heard he poached the job as the official festival bookstore." Zen sniffed. "I can't imagine him taking as much care with his selections as you have, Mina. All that work you put in...I'm hopping mad on your behalf. I wish that man had never moved to the village—oh, I'm sorry, Shelley. I didn't mean to speak ill of your dad. I know you must be happy to have him around for Max."

I jumped, feeling guilty to be caught badmouthing Shelley's father in front of her, even if he deserved every word.

"That's okay, Zen, Mina," Shelley said as she emerged from the doorway to chase her son out from under the costume rack. "I actually came over to apologize for the way he's barged in and taken over the festival. I'm so embarrassed by—Max, *stop that.*"

I winced as something crashed, and Max giggled. Shelley scooped the wriggling toddler into her arms. "I'm sorry about this little terror. Dad was *supposed* to take Max to the park today, but he's too busy in his shop even though he has Mr. Delacroix to manage it for him, so I had to bring him along with me. I thought when Dad moved to Argleton it was because he wanted us to be a proper family, but he doesn't seem to care about anything unless it has old pages and a huge price tag."

"I'm sure once Mr. Rasmussen is used to having you and Max in his life, he'll warm up," I said, although I secretly thought she was right.

"Or he'll remain a cad of the first order," Morrie quipped. "That's also a possibility."

"I think Mr. Moriarty is right. Anyway," Shelley said. "I'm going to try to talk to him about donating the book to the museum. It's what I'd do if I ran his store. And let's just say, I think he's finally going to be forced to listen to me."

Another crash. This time, I distinctly heard Puck yell, "Do that again, young fiend, and I shall fix an ass's nole upon your head."

"*Puck*, don't you dare turn that baby into a donkey—"

CRASH.

"Waaaah!"

"Mina, is everything going okay in here?" Miles Shackleton stepped into the middle of the chaos, blocking Morrie as he was about to spring on Puck. "I heard something break."

Shelley grabbed Max and scampered away. Puck transformed into his pixie form and hid in the makeup case, and Zen picked up her purse and hurried to the bathroom to change. I rubbed my temple, where the first twitches of a headache were starting to form. "Everything is under control, Miles. We're ready for opening night."

"Good." His shoulders visibly sagged with relief. "I was just coming to tell you the good news. Well, it's good, but also a bit terrifying. I've just got off the phone with our promoter in London, and she said that with the First Folio on display, the press are beating down her door for tickets to opening night. We're going to be in every major news outlet in England."

"That's awesome, Miles."

"It is, isn't it?" He gripped the back of a makeup chair so hard his fingers dug into the fabric. "She also tells me that a group of investors has booked out the last Lord's Room tomorrow. If they like what they see, they might be interested in funding the New New Globe's national tour. It's the dream, Mina. It's the dream."

"I'm excited for all of us." I beamed at him. I was happy the theater was getting such positive attention. Miles had poured so much into this project. He'd been planning the construction of the New New Globe for over a year, poring over old documents and scholarly articles with Zen to create a design that reflected the Elizabethan theater experience and could be easily set up, packed down, and moved. He deserved for the festival to be a raging success.

Miles' voice softened. "Mina, I know you must be sad about not doing the festival bookshop any longer, but none of this would've happened without Mr. Rasmussen and his First Folio. Having that book on display in the village is a real coup."

"I understand. It's business." I choked a little on the word. "I'm happy to help out with costumes and whatever else you need."

"Good, good." He ran his fingers through his curly black hair, which looked like it could do with a shampoo. Come to think of it, everything about Miles seemed a bit rumpled and frazzled. And he smelt like Heathcliff's bedroom when the wind changed. "Our job now is to make sure everything runs absolutely perfectly so we take a crowbar to these investors' wallets and jimmy them open."

"Poor Miles," I said when he left. "He seems bedraggled."

"He should be," Morrie said. "He's mortgaged his house on the success of this festival."

"What?" *That's insane.* Miles lived in a beautiful old Georgian estate outside the village – the kind of property anyone with good taste and no sense would dream of owning. "How do you know that?"

"It's my business to know things."

I made a face at Morrie. "It legitimately isn't."

"Fine, then. It's my criminal nature that wants to know things. And I know that Miles Stapleton has his entire personal fortune riding on the success of the festival and the New New Globe, and his wife has no idea. If *anything* goes wrong with the festival, he'll be ruined."

CHAPTER FOUR

"*I*'ll take all of these, thank you." The man dropped what looked like every Stella Mey book we stocked onto the counter.

"So you're a big Stella Mey fan, are you?" I smiled as I rang up the books. "Me too. I love the way she twisted the vampire trope and made it her own. I just adored *Dusk*."

"I've never heard of her." The man's eyes gleamed with a weird kind of hunger as he grabbed the books out of my hands the moment I'd scanned them. Was he afraid someone he knew might see him with his teen vampire books?

Customers are weird.

"There you go. Your total is £18.29." As he counted out notes and coins into my hand, I held out a program. "While you're here in the village, why don't you check out the Argleton Shakespeare Festival—"

"Shakespeare?" the customer scoffed. "Isn't he the fellow with the plays? Who needs that nonsense now that we have the telly?"

Heathcliff nodded at Quoth. "Take it, bird."

I'm on it.

The man snatched his receipt from my hand, muttered something like 'this had better be worth it,' and stormed out. Quoth flapped down from the chandelier and swooped into the hallway after him. A moment later, the customer bellowed.

"Argh. That poxy bird shat on me!"

The man poked his head around the corner. Quoth must've been saving up for someone special, because there was such a quantity of bird poop dripping down the side of his face I could see it from all the way across the room. Quoth fluttered back in and perched on the till, peering up at me with those fire-rimmed eyes.

Bullseye, he declared inside my head.

I burst out laughing. From across the room, a customer browsing the Victorian section cracked up into her book. My laughter died on my lips. Even though the man was rude, we shouldn't be laughing at customers in front of other people. That was a fine way to end up as the bookshop with the *reputation*. And we already had a reputation for strange friends in odd costumes hanging around, a surly proprietor, a cheeky raven, and a penchant for getting embroiled in murders.

The man stormed off, yelling that we'd hear from his lawyer. The girl who laughed approached the counter.

"I'm sorry," she said as she held out a book. "I didn't mean to laugh, it's just…you know, *bullseye*, and he kind of looked like an angry bull…"

I peered at her, my eyes wide. *How does she know Quoth said the word bullseye?*

It's almost as if she…

…heard what Quoth said.

But that's impossible.

No one, and I mean *no one*, had ever shown indication that they could hear Quoth's thoughts when he was in his raven form. Other literary characters could, and I could because I was the daughter of Homer with the waters of Meles in my veins, but this random customer…

I squinted at this girl with perfectly straightened hair and a sweatshirt covered in tiny, googly-eyed bats, trying to figure out what was going on. I squinted so long that I didn't notice she was still holding out her book like a peace offering.

"Sorry." I waved my hands around like a madwoman. "Blind girl moment. Can I help you?"

"Okay if I leave these here?" The girl dropped the volume on the desk in front of me and piled some more books on top of it. "I want to go upstairs and get some more books, and these are heavy."

"Sure. Go right ahead."

She set down her books and flounced away. She turned at the doorway and said in a low voice. "We'll get you a military strategy book, I promise. Hold on a sec, I've got to check out the travel section first."

"Huh, what was that?"

"Oh." Her voice thickened with embarrassment. "Nothing. It was nothing. I talk to myself sometimes, is all."

Okay, sure. There's talking to yourself, which we all do, and then there's having an argument with yourself and hearing a magical raven inside your head and not being fazed at all, *which is a complete other kettle of fish.*

I have to know what's going on with this girl.

"I'm taking a break." I dropped her books into Heathcliff's arms, thrust Oscar at him, and slid around the desk. I tiptoed across the rug to reach the bottom of the stairs just as the girl stepped on the creaky floorboard at the top.

Feeling like a dark romance anti-hero, I crept up the stairs after her, keeping to the shadows and placing my feet on the places where I knew the floorboards don't creak. Normally, I couldn't navigate without Oscar, but I knew every corner of Nevermore by heart. I reached the top of the stairs and turned to the nearest shelf, pretending to rearrange the titles as silently as possible while I watched her through a gap in the books.

We'd installed enough lamps up here that I could make out shapes across the room. The girl moved around between the shelves, stopping occasionally to pull out books and hold them up as if examining the covers. She kept up a steady stream of muttered conversation. She was talking to herself except that... except that this wasn't insane rambling. It was more like she was having an argument with someone invisible, someone I couldn't hear.

I might have written her off as one of the strange customers we get inside the bookshop, except that I was positive she heard Quoth.

Who is she talking to? Is it possible that I'm not the only person with the waters of Meles in my veins—

"Excuse me, ma'am."

I leaped out of my skin, knocking books all over the floor. I turned to see a middle-aged man peering at me through the books. "Don't mind me. I'm just...uh...stroking these books." I shoved my hands into the shelf and start shuffling them back and forth, my face going beet red as I felt the girl's eyes burning into my back. *She knows I came up here to spy on her.* "If you don't show them a bit of love every now and then, they get ornery."

"Right. Yes." The man peered at me through horn-rimmed glasses like he was safer taking his question to Heathcliff. Which he very definitely was not. "I have a very important question that must be dealt with in haste. Do you have any books by Stella Mey?"

CHAPTER FIVE

"*H*ave no fear, good peasants," Morrie yelled as he burst through the stage doors. "Macbeth is in the house."

Puck spluttered out an Elizabethan insult and disappeared in a flurry of sparkles. The few other cast members still scattered around the room going over their lines or drinking quietly while Quoth and I worked, grabbed their coats, and shuffled outside, muttering under their breath about curses and inferior understudies.

"Why did you do that?" I asked, rubbing my eyes as flicks of green and orange light danced over my vision. *It must be getting late.* "You know it annoys everyone."

"I'm helping. I am the most helpful." Morrie grabbed my hand. "They all needed to go home and get a good night's sleep before the opening showcase. And besides, I have something to show you both and I wanted absolute privacy."

"But I've still got to hem these pantaloons—"

"Put down the pincushion, gorgeous." Morrie's voice carried that quiet authority that never failed to make my knees weak. I did exactly as he commanded. "Relinquish your paintbrush, birdie. And come with me."

We followed Morrie through the stage door onto the stage itself. The New New Globe was shrouded in darkness, the seats eerily empty. Morrie had been working out here with the backstage crew most of the day. As well as understudy for Macbeth, he designed all the special effects for the plays, using his mathematical skills to create cunning illusions that would thrill a modern audience but keep our actors completely safe.

Morrie gestured to a spotlighted area of the stage, which was, as far as this blind girl could tell, completely empty. "Ta-da!"

"You finished it?" Quoth's voice rose with excitement.

"Yup." Morrie jumped on the spot a couple of times. "See? It's perfectly secure. You can't even notice the trapdoor is here."

"There's a trapdoor?" I asked.

"But of course. It's for lowering Juliet into her tomb. Personally, I think it's a little too *Hammer Horror*, but Mrs. Ellis wanted a grand finale." Morrie led Quoth to a dark corner of the stage and tapped something on the floor with the tip of his brogue. "This is the lever that operates the trapdoor. One hard stomp and it will fly open, but I'll have Juliet all rigged up so she won't hurt herself."

"May I try it?"

"Of course. Stand well back, gorgeous." Morrie shuffled me away from the spotlights.

Quoth gave the lever a hard stomp and a square of the stage flew open. I cried out in delight. It was such a shock. The audience would *freak*.

"Morrie, that's pretty amazing. You can't tell it's there at all." I moved a little closer and peered down into 'hell' (what Shakespearean actors called the area below the stage) but I couldn't see anything except a deep, dark pit.

"Of course it's amazing. I designed it. And that's not the only special effects apparatus I completed today." Morrie's voice carried a hint of mischief. He led me and Quoth up to the third-floor gallery, turning on just enough of the lights that I could find my way. He gestured to a small platform on the very edge of the gallery, directly over the groundlings below and accessed via a locked gate. Attached to the platform was a complex-looking tangle of ropes and pulleys and leather stirrups.

"What's this?"

"It's the rigging that will enable Lady Macbeth to throw herself off the castle walls without breaking her pretty neck." Morrie unlocked the gate and yanked the ropes toward him. "It's all designed to be invisible under her clothing. And perfectly safe, of course. I've tested this for many times her weight and in all possible scenarios. But for tonight, I've made some very specific adjustments. Mina, would you like to demonstrate?"

"I don't know if that's a good idea." I bit my lip. Just because I couldn't see the three-story drop below me didn't mean I wanted to be suspended above it on some flimsy wires, no matter how much I trusted Morrie's mathematical genius.

"It might be fun," Quoth said, a strange tone creeping into his voice. "You'll feel like you're flying."

I smiled at him. Flying was something we talked about a lot, because he got to do it every day and I'd desperately love to have wings. "You're right. Okay, how do I get in this thing? I put this loop over my thigh, right? And this one…"

"No, no," Morrie's arms went around my stomach, and his tongue flicked over my neck. "I said I made some *special* adjustments. You're going to have to be naked."

"Um…" I stared at the contraption again, at the straps and loops and stirrups that would hold a person with their legs *wide apart in the air*, and it *hit* me.

Morrie had turned the rigging into a sex swing.

Of course he fucking had.

A blush crept over my skin, from my toes right up to my skull.

Morrie is crazy. We can't just mess around with this equipment. It's not designed for what he wants...

But obviously it was, because James Moriarty designed it with just such mischief and shenanigans in mind.

Morrie's body folded around me, and he pressed his chest into my back. His hardness brushed my thigh as his hands wandered over my chest, lightly touching, teasing, drawing me into this fantasy he'd orchestrated. He did so love being the puppetmaster, and he was finally going to hook me up to strings.

He undid my shirt buttons one by one as he laid a trail of kisses along my neck. His fingers brushed my skin, trailing lines of fire – little sparks that flitted and burst. He slid his hands under my bra and pushed it up. Cool air rushed from below to kiss my nipples, drawing them into hard points.

Adrenaline surged in my veins. *I'm standing on the edge of a sheer drop, and Morrie can still make me feel like this.*

"I know you're curious, gorgeous," he whispered against my skin as he cupped my breasts, fingertips teasing my hard nipples. "I can tell by the way your lips part ever so slightly, and your breathing – so quick and shallow as your little heart races. You want this. It's a simple deduction."

"But one of the cast members might see us," I moaned my final objection as Morrie rolled my nipple in his fingers, adding the slightest pinch – a little pain to draw out the pleasure.

"Precisely why I scared everyone away." Morrie kissed my shoulders as he folded down the fabric, tugging my arms out of the sleeves, slow and deliberate, drawing out the undressing for his own pleasure. "Curses do have their benefits. There's no one here but you and me and Quoth."

Quoth. What does he...

Quoth moved closer, leaning on the gallery railing. His eyes raked over me as Morrie dropped my shirt and bra into the groundlings.

"Morrie, what are you trying to do to her?" His voice choked with emotion.

"I thought it was obvious. I'm trying to get Mina's clothes off. Care to help?"

Quoth did love to help. He practically skipped over, stepping onto the edge of the narrow platform to reach for me. Morrie lifted me under my shoulders while Quoth slid off my fishnet stockings and my red tartan skirt. Their fingers brushed my skin, the sensation mingling with the adrenaline coursing through me to make my blood pulse and my head light.

Morrie grabbed my hips and lifted me off the ground, settling my ass into the narrow leather sling, while Quoth threaded my legs and arms through the loops and stirrups. When they'd finished, they stepped back, and the swing rocked. My stomach dropped away as I swung out over the theater, suspended three stories up with only Morrie's contraption keeping me from plunging to my death.

I took a moment to breathe, to focus on the new sensations flooding my body – the tug and pinch of the rigging around my legs and arms, the cool kiss of the air rushing up beneath me, the stretch in my muscles of my legs held wide, the ache between my thighs, begging to be filled.

Morrie's voice dripped with lust. "You look amazing, Mina. Don't you agree, birdie?"

"Uh." Quoth didn't seem to know how to form words.

Morrie gave the swing a little nudge with his brogue. As I swung, cool air wafted over my body, pebbling my nipples, caressing between my legs, like the ghost of a kiss. I moaned as the room spun, the lights twirling and swimming in my vision.

"She's all yours, birdie," Morrie said. "I thought it was time you both got to fly."

Quoth stepped up onto the platform. I swung just in front of him, close enough I could make out the silhouette of his body and hear the tiny gasp he made as he watched me. He trailed his fingers down my legs, warm and gentle and reverent. Breath hissed from his lips. I arched toward him, but that only made me swing away.

Eeeee. By Isis, this is quite fun.

Quoth grabbed hold of one of the stirrups, holding me still so I bobbed in mid-air just in front of him. He pushed the very tip of his finger inside me, teasing my entrance. I groaned as the ache in my belly grew. I tried to buck my hips toward him, but I couldn't move in the swing, couldn't even close my legs an inch to increase the pressure. All I could do was float and soar while I grew wetter and the fire stoked inside me.

He leaned over and kissed the skin above my belly button, his fingers darting, stroking, never giving me enough pressure. I growled.

"You're teasing me."

In response, Quoth tapped the swing away. I swang out, crying with frustration as his touch disappeared. But when I returned, I plunged straight onto his finger.

Fuuuuuuuuck yes.

Quoth kept the swing moving so that every time I swung back toward him it drove his finger deeper. He curled his thumb upward to play with my clit, slamming the pad onto the sensitive bud with each rock of the swing. I gasped and jerked, but I was completely trapped, unable to do anything but enjoy this slow and impossible torture.

He rubbed his thumb in a circle on my clit and pushed a second finger inside. Something about not being able to move, about being stuck in this awkward position with my head back and my legs spread wide, and his languid pace that demanded I feel every stroke, every movement, every creak and rock of the swing, drove me to the brink and over the edge, and I was falling and I was flying into the sun, into the greatest, hardest, most intense orgasm I'd ever had.

Someone was screaming. It took me a few moments to come back to earth and realize the screamer was me.

You ever had an orgasm while flying? Yeah, I highly recommend it.

But Quoth wasn't done yet. With a cry like a wounded animal, he grabbed my thighs and impaled me onto his shaft. I couldn't do anything – couldn't push back or move my hips or draw away. He was in complete control of my body and the swing. It was so strange to feel so helpless and yet, so utterly adored.

He wrapped one hand around my head, his fingers threading through my hair as he controlled the rocking and brought me to him for a deep, searing kiss. The other hand gripped my thigh, his nails digging so hard I wouldn't be surprised if they drew blood. He leaned down to suck a nipple into his mouth and I was gone again, flying somewhere above my body.

I came – a shuddering, screaming mess on his cock. When I orgasm, my thighs want to clamp together, almost like the sensation is too much. But I couldn't do that on the swing, I couldn't move my thighs at all. I had to endure every sensation as my skin became a thousand tiny matchsticks all being struck at once.

Quoth rocked his hips, sending me swinging and slamming me back into him. The leather stirrups pinched my thighs, and it felt so fucking amazing. Quoth cried out as his body tensed, as his cock jerked and hardened inside me, and in his cry I heard the pain and guilt he'd carried with him for so long, and I hoped he could let it fly away and never bother him again.

I thought I orgasmed once more, but I didn't know because I was fucking *flying*.

"What about you?" I asked Morrie, my voice thick with lust.

"Not today," he said as he helped me down and made sure I was well away from the edge, since my legs didn't work yet. "This was a gift for him. But it didn't have quite the effect I desired."

I turned toward where Morrie was looking, to where Quoth

hurried away down the stairs, his head bowed and his waterfall of dark hair flailing around him.

I knew without asking exactly what Morrie was thinking. *If Mina in a sex swing can't cheer Quoth up, what will?*

And I wished more than I'd wished for anything in my whole life that I had the answer.

CHAPTER SIX

"Heathcliff, hurry up. I need you down here," I called up the stairs, my hand poised on the CLOSED sign. Oscar pawed at the rug, eager to begin the day. He loved being a shop dog, tugging his little red cart of books around to help me stack the shelves, and greeting all the customers. But we couldn't open without Heathcliff – I needed him to price new stock so Oscar and I could man the counter. Or woman and dog the counter.

"I know what we can do while we wait." Quoth slapped my hand down on the sign and swept me into his arms. His lips brushed mine, lighting my body on fire. For a moment, I considered leaving the shop shut and spending the day in bed with my birdie.

But as much as I was keen for a little Quoth time, I knew that several busloads of tourists would be arriving in the village for the festival. We might not be the official Shakespeare bookseller, and we didn't have a fancypants First Folio to draw in a crowd, but people would wander all over the village, and they'd be drawn into our friendly (ish) and cozy (dusty) bookshop. I'd set out our Shakespeare books in an attractive display, and even roped Puck into running a fairy story-time for the children. Nevermore Bookshop may be down, but we weren't out.

"Heathcliff," I yelled, as Quoth nibbled on my ear. *Urge to open shop, fading, fading...*

"Here," Heathcliff barked. He stomped down the stairs and waved something white in my face.

"What's this?"

"It's my ruffle. You'll have to fasten it."

I grinned as Quoth transformed and fluttered up to his perch over the door. I wrapped the ruffle around Heathcliff's neck and secured it tightly at the back.

Nyuh-nyuh-nyuh, Quoth laughed as he peered down at Heathcliff. I had to choke back a laugh of my own. With his broad shoulders and swarthy features, Heathcliff looked like a pissed-off Tiffany lamp.

Heathcliff's face twisted, and he reached up to yank off the ruffle.

"Don't listen to him. You look handsome." I kissed the tip of Heathcliff's nose.

"I look like a doily," he muttered as he moved into the main room. "I am a candle, the better burnt out."

He really loves that insult book, Quoth said inside my head.

I couldn't stop grinning as I checked the window displays one last time and flicked over the CLOSED sign to OPEN.

Let the Argleton Shakespeare Festival begin.

Quoth and I sat in the bay window and watched the first busloads of tourists arrive on the village green. They meandered around the quaint shops and showed off their festival bags. A line formed outside Rasmussen Books, and the smarmy proprietor sat in a booth beside the entrance, taking two quid per person as an entrance fee (I mean, come *on*) and waving people inside. His business partner, that lanky fellow Lawrence Delacroix, led each guest around the shop, no doubt regaling them with tales from when he was a Shakespearean actor and giving them a sales pitch for their expensive collector's editions alongside their history lesson.

The line had become a mini-festival of its own. Earl showed up with a lute he'd made from old car parts, and entertained with bawdy songs while tourists in costumes danced around the green. Richard sold them traditional meat pies and sandwiches, and Mrs. Ellis hopped up and down the line with Morrie and Puck and a couple of the other actors in full costume, hand-selling tickets to tonight's grand opening.

It looked like so much fun, and I bet many people in the line would be interested in our books. And yet, we couldn't participate. We were no longer the "official" bookseller. We had to hang back and let Rasmussen's First Folio Fever take over *our* town.

"I really hate Rasmussen," Quoth said. He'd eaten his breakfast of berries and transformed back into his human form. Usually, Quoth didn't like being in the shop in his human form if there were a lot of people around, but it didn't look like it would be an issue today.

"Agreed. He shouldn't make people pay just to go inside his shop."

But people *were* paying. By lunchtime, the line of people waiting to get their glimpse of Rasmussen's First Folio snaked around the green and blocked the entrance to the pub. A few wandered into Nevermore after they'd had their fill of staring at old, expensive books and wanted to look at some old, cheap ones, instead. We sold a handful of items from our prominent Shakespeare display, but nothing like what we would have sold if Rasmussen had never shown his face in the village.

Not that I was bitter or anything.

Not at all.

We tried to distract ourselves from what was going on out in the square. Morrie and I played chess. Quoth worked on a painting. Heathcliff yelled at the radio. Puck entertained ten kids by turning one of their teachers into a donkey. The children squealed with delight and didn't seem to notice that when they left the store, their teacher was still only talking in hee-haws.

At 3PM, the shop bell rang. I was listening to an interesting audiobook, so I left the customer to browse. But a few moments later, I felt a presence on the other side of the desk.

"Hey, did you see what's going on in the square?" someone asked. I paused my audiobook and looked up to see the girl from the other day – the one who was having arguments with herself. Today, she wore a wool dress that hugged her curves and a necklace on a leather thong that looked like it might've been a Roman coin.

My surprise must've shown on my face, because she waved her hand in the air. "Sorry. I didn't mean to startle you. I'm surprised it's so quiet in here. I would have thought this festival would attract lots of people to a bookshop."

"You'd think." I tried not to sound bitter. "They're all lining up at Rasmussen Books to see the First Folio. Our perfectly-ordinary *popular books* can't compete."

"If it's any consolation, I went there this morning and your bookshop is much cooler. And you don't charge admission or have a gangly fellow follow you around the store to make sure you don't steal anything."

"Were you at least allowed to take photos?"

"Only if you pay an extra pound." She held up her phone. "What can I say? Got my selfie with the big bad book. I'm a sucker for an Instagram pic."

"Can I see?"

She didn't ask why a blind girl wanted to look at photographs, which made me like her seven million times more. I took the phone from her and held it under the light, close enough to my face that my nose was practically touching. There she was, smiling up at the camera, with the book open in a velvet-lined cradle behind her. It showed the first page of 'Much Ado About Nothing,' with a beautiful floral border.

Something stabbed at my stomach. I'd actually love to see the First Folio. But no way was I stepping inside Rasmussen's shop. I handed the phone back. "Love it. You should make that your dating profile pic. You know, 'My Folio bringeth all the boys to the yard—"

"And they're like, it's better than thine—"

I laughed. "Verily, it's better than thine—"

"—I could teach you, but I must levy a fee'," she finished with a snort. "I'm Bree, by the way."

"I'm Mina. And this is Oscar." Bree smiled down at Oscar but didn't go to pet him. She obviously knew he was working. "You were in here the other day."

"Yeah. I live in Grimdale, just over the valley. Well, I've only just moved back. I grew up there but I've lived all over – Canada, Germany, Vietnam, New Zealand. I don't like to stay in the same place for long, but my parents need me to housesit for them while they grand tour around Europe for their retirement. Grimdale is *boring*. It's dead. Deadly dead. No action whatsoever. We don't even have a bookshop. Hence why I'm back – I need more reading material."

"I'm an Argleton native. I know all about village life," I laughed. "Maybe I can recommend something. What do you like to read?"

"Travel biographies. And, um, historical accounts of famous battles. Anything by…Julius Caesar. I adore him. Um, and anything about overthrowing the monarchy." She bent her head to the side before looking back at me. "I mean, *embroidery*. Anything about embroidery."

"That's…a diverse range of interests."

"Yes, well, I like reading. And apparently, embroidery." Bree's laugh sounded kind of forced. "Anything to silence the voices in my head."

I showed Bree some of our popular travel books, and she brought a stack. When she handed over her money, she muttered, "No, I don't know how much that is in denarii." But apart from that, she seemed sort-of normal. I wanted to ask her if she'd like to go for a drink at the pub, but I chickened out.

"Thanks again." Bree accepted her bag of books from me. "Hey, are you going to the opening ceremony tonight?"

"I wouldn't miss it. My boyfriend is playing Macbeth, and my mum is one of the three witches."

"Fun. I might see you there. I was thinking of heading along. It's no Burning Man, but it'll be good for a laugh." She nodded at me as she whipped out her phone. "Hey, what's your number? I'll text you mine. Maybe we could go for a drink sometime? When you're not busy?"

"Yeah." I grinned at her. "I'd love that."

*A*t 4PM, we shut up shop, and I went upstairs to change into my outfit for the opening ceremony. I figured that the costume designer needed to set the scene for the festival, so I spent every night this week sewing myself a beautiful Elizabethan corset that squished my tiny boobs up into a rather impressive cleavage. I paired this with skintight wet-look leggings, a cage skirt in an Elizabethan shape that Quoth helped me construct, and my favorite Docs.

"Arf." Oscar sat in front of the mirror while I changed.

I patted his head. "Don't worry, boy. I have your costume right here."

As I tied Oscar's ruffle around his collar and added his jester-bells to his harness, Quoth came down from his room. He wore his usual black dress shirt, his raven hair falling over his shoulders in a silken waterfall. He made a choking noise when he saw me. His arms went around my waist, and he pulled me close.

"You look like a dream," he whispered. "I was never insane, except upon occasions like this when my heart is touched by you."

"Yeah, yeah. You talk so pretty, but you don't look too shabby yourself." I grazed his lips with mine. Quoth looped his fingers into the cage and yanked me forward, crushing me against him. His lips devoured mine, hot and hungry.

I responded by drawing up against him and kissing him deeper, raking my fingers through his hair. Quoth feathered kisses over my lips, my neck, my jawline, tasting my skin like he was struck by some mystery illness and I was the only medicine.

My birdie. I missed you.

This was the first time since I brought him back that Quoth had touched me like this, his fingers dancing over my curves and brushing the edge of my breast. As his lips found mine again and our tongues entwined, I tasted Quoth as I always knew him, stripped of the guilt he'd carried for too long. He'd let all that pain fall away to reveal the beautiful soul beneath.

And he wasn't the only one stripped bare by the magic of our connection. As I sank into Quoth's arms, all the stress of the last couple of days melted away. *We can be a little late for the opening. I can take him back upstairs and let him unlock this cage and...*

"Who's this, so wither'd and so wild in his attire, that he looks not like the inhabitants of the earth, and yet is on it?"

Shakespearean quotes weren't uncommon in this bookshop, but for Heathcliff Earnshaw to speak with such strangled wonderment...I tore my lips from Quoth, looked up, and choked on my tongue.

Heathcliff stood in the doorway to his room, dressed in a dark suit that accentuated his broad shoulders and wild obsidian eyes. He was turned toward the end of the hall, where several lamps illuminated Morrie posing in all his glory in his Scottish kilt, the sword I used to slay Dracula swinging in his long fingers.

"Out of my sight." Heathcliff declared, waving his hands at the kilt. "Thou dost infect my eyes."

"Why, my fair prince, the tartness of your face could sour ripe grapes." Morrie pinned Heathcliff's arm to the wall and stepped in to kiss him roughly. Heathcliff yelped in protest but yielded his lips, and the pair of them fought against each other for the upper hand as their kiss heated up until the air around us sizzled with invisible fire.

"We should…get…to the opening…" I gasped as Quoth kissed his way down my neck. His hand slid down between my thighs, teasing me through the fabric of my leggings. I could feel how wet I'd become.

"Yes, yes. We wouldn't want to be late. That would be so terribly naughty of us. Besides, there's a bit of a draft in here." Morrie slid away from Heathcliff and stuck his leg up on the table, wiggling his hips to give Heathcliff a view under his kilt.

"What are you wearing?" Heathcliff stared at Morrie in horror, although I could tell his voice thickened with desire. Quoth's fingers stroked me faster, pressing into me through the fabric.

"This is my costume for the play," Morrie preened, holding the edges of his kilt and doing a curtsey. "Mina made it, and it's wonderful. Even though I'm not performing tonight, I want everyone in the festival to know the handsome, devilish rogue who will play Macbeth."

"And how many times do you plan to say the word 'Macbeth' tonight?" I asked, my words breathless as Quoth's finger danced fiery pleasure between my legs. My knees wobbled.

"About three dozen." Morrie held out his arm for me. "Come, come, you two saucy knaves, we mustn't keep our adoring public waiting."

"One moment," Quoth said. He reached around and tipped my

chin back, bending his head to plunge his tongue deep into my mouth as he drilled his finger in a fast circle. I cried out into his lips as my legs collapsed and a hot wave coursed through my veins, turning my brain into mush and my limbs to jelly.

"Tsk, tsk," Morrie tutted as he helped Quoth stand me on my feet again. "Mina, I'm surprised at you, fooling around when we have a very important event to attend. What if someone's murdered tonight and we're not there to solve it?"

"The only person being murdered is you, after you make all the actors perform the Scottish Play Curse Dance seventeen times." I slapped Morrie on the shoulder as I picked up Oscar's harness, aware as I descended the stairs that all three of my boyfriends were walking rather stiffly.

Please let the opening go without a hitch. Please let the worst thing that happens tonight be a serious case of blue balls. I cannot deal with any more murders right now.

CHAPTER SEVEN

*P*uck waited at the bottom of the stairs for us, dressed in his costume. I'd attired him in green velvet, with leaf shapes accentuating his arms and shoulders. He'd twisted vines and flowers in his hair, and if he didn't have that mischievous fairy glint in his eye, I'd almost think he was cute.

"How now spirit, wither wander you?" he greeted me.

"Get him away from me," my grandmother called from somewhere in the gloom. "I'll scratch his eyes out. I'll unravel the wool on his favorite sweater. I'll tear off his tongue and chew it and puke it up on the rug and then eat it again—"

I glared at Puck. "What did you do to her?"

"This woman's an easy glove," he shot back, quoting Lafeu from *All's Well That Ends Well*, because apparently everyone was reading Heathcliff's Shakespearean insult book. "She goes off and on at pleasure."

"Of course she does. She's a cat. But what did you *do* to her?"

"I was minding my own business, chasing a piece of string under the shelves, and he turned the string into a snake." Grimalkin cried, "It bit my nose!"

I leaned over, flipping the edge of the tablecloth. From the gloom, a pair of yellow eyes glared back at me, and I could just make out the slope of my grandmother's shoulders, and she waited to pounce.

"It really hurts," Grimalkin complained.

"Justice always whirls in equal measure," Puck shot back. "She placed a dead mouse upon my pillow."

"And I'll do much worse." Grimalkin tore the corner of the tablecloth from my grip. A moment later, a black cat streaked toward us. She planted all four feet on the rug and glared up at Puck, her back arched, fur fluffed up, and let out a wild hiss.

Puck ducked and made a run for the door. Grimalkin tore after him, swiping at his heels with extended claws.

"Let's away, 'ere break of day," Puck cried out as he ran into the street.

"You read my mind." Heathcliff held out his arm, and I held onto his elbow as we walked out into the night. Morrie came out next, whistling as he swung his sword through the air. Quoth closed and locked the shop and fell in step beside me, fitting his hand into mine.

Puck hobbled in front of us, holding his ankle where Grimalkin had slashed him. My grandmother sat on the awning over Oliver's bakery, licking her paws with the self-satisfaction only a cat could exude.

We walked up Butcher Street and hurried across the green. The village was mostly in darkness – everyone had already left for the New New Globe – but under the streetlamps I could see Mr. Rasmussen shooing away the stragglers who were still waiting for their peek at the First Folio.

"I really hate that man," I said.

"He has sailed into the north of my lady's opinion," Heathcliff added. "Where he hangs like an icicle on a Dutchman's beard."

"That's a good one," Morrie said. *Twelfth Night?*

Heathcliff nodded proudly.

"Want me to cast a spell upon him?" Puck cut in. "I could turn him into a toad. Or a walrus. Or perchance I could make him fall in love with you. I am rather good at love spells. Then he'll do whatever you say."

I shuddered. "Thanks, Puck, but we don't need magic to solve this problem. Nevermore Bookshop isn't afraid of a little friendly competition."

"Agreed," Morrie said. "But we're also not above a little friendly sabotage."

Morrie and Puck spent the rest of the way to the school suggesting progressively more elaborate methods of revenge against Rasmussen and his bookstore. Even Heathcliff chimed in with a few diabolical propositions, mostly involving Rasmussen's testicles and various medieval torture devices. Quoth and I walked a little behind the others, Oscar trotting obediently in front of me.

I laid my head on Quoth's shoulder. "I know they're all worried about Rasmussen," I said. "But I'm worried about you."

"Please don't be." He squeezed my hand. "I'm perfectly content."

"Are you, though? Quoth, you went through a harrowing experience with Dracula, and you can smile that beautiful smile of yours and say that you're okay, but that doesn't make it true. Your body wasn't your own. What Dracula did to you was an invasion, and you can't keep blaming yourself—"

"Mina, I'm perfectly okay."

"I don't think you are. I think you'd feel better if you talked to someone—"

"There's no therapist for fictional characters," Quoth said. "And even if there were, I wouldn't have anything to say. You and Morrie and Heathcliff and the shop are all I need."

"You blame yourself," I whispered. "I see you doing it. I hear it in your voice. You believe what happened was your fault."

"It *was* my fault."

He said it so simply, so without hope or yearning, that I knew it was a truth he utterly believed. And that made tears prick at the corners of my eyes.

"No, Quoth, it wasn't. You cannot bear the guilt that falls on Dracula's shoulders. He manipulated so many people. Think about Grey Lachlan and all those horrible things he did under Dracula's spell. No one blames him for them, because he wasn't himself. Even when we were at the art gallery and you attacked me…I knew it wasn't you. You were trying to fight his power, and in the end, you gave your own life to save me. I never needed to forgive you because there's nothing to forgive, but you have to find a way to forgive yourself."

"I try. I get up every day and I promise myself that today will be better, that I'll do so much good that I'll be able to look at myself in the mirror without wanting to scratch my own eyes out. But the truth is that people *died* because of what I did, because I felt lonely and useless and that I had nothing of value to offer you or anyone. And he came along and made me feel wanted, so I became the person I most feared I was inside and…" Quoth's sad words trailed off as he stared ahead, and his pace quickened. "Mina, can you see it? It looks beautiful."

"I can!" We'd arrived at the edge of the school field. The theater had been strung with colorful fairy lights, which meant that I could actually make out the lines of its shape in the night. All around us, people chatted excitedly about the plays and the First Folio as they enjoyed cider in the beer garden. We strolled past the line of people waiting to be seated and straight up the secret staircase behind the stage, with Morrie and Puck leading the way.

The New New Globe consisted of three levels of gallery seating arranged in a circle around the rectangular wooden stage. The gallery seats were for richer patrons of Shakespeare's day who often paid extra for a cushion to make the wooden benches more comfortable. Galleries above the stage wall – called Lord's Rooms – allowed the nobility to look down upon the actors from above and be seen by everyone in attendance. In front of the stage, in the middle of the circle, was the yard, where 'groundlings' tickets were sold for one penny to anyone wishing to stand and watch the play. The groundlings sounded like the place to be to me, right up close and personal with the actors, and that's where we'd be watching most of the performances. Action on stage often spilled over into the yard – like the mosh pits I was used to from punk and metal shows.

But tonight, we had reserved special tickets. Morrie skipped ahead and threw open the door to the first Lord's Room. "After you, m'lady."

Oscar led the way inside, directing me to a velvet-cushioned chair right by the window that overlooked the stage.

"This is so cool." I leaned out the window. The stage lights illuminated Quoth's colorful sets and the crowd gathering in the groundlings and circular galleries. I'd have to crane my neck to look down at the actors, who would face away from us out into the theater, but I couldn't see much anyway so that was fine by me. I'd much rather feel like Elizabethan royalty for a night with my three boyfriends and my dog and a troublesome fairy.

A heavy figure sat down beside me, and a plate of food wafted under my nose. "Mrs. Ellis left us a decent spread," Heathcliff said as he held up a tiny meat pie for me to taste. "I've always said how much I like that old bint."

"You've said no such thing," I teased him as I opened my mouth to accept the treat. Mrs. Ellis had gone all out for the opening ceremony, with a charcuterie board containing Argleton cheeses and Richard's own smoked sausage, and tiny chocolate brownies and scones from Oliver's bakery.

Heathcliff shifted in his chair, and I knew he was still thinking about what happened back at the flat. We were going to have a hard time (sorry, such a Morrie joke) keeping our hands off each other during the two-hour show.

Heathcliff moved his chair closer and set the plate down on

my lap so he could throw his arm around my shoulders. "There's your friend from the shop in the front row. The one who talks to herself."

"Her name is Bree." I waved in the general direction I thought he was pointing. I couldn't make out faces from this far away.

"You just greeted the pillar," Heathcliff said. I snorted. You have to have a sense of humor about going blind.

"Look who's got the box right next to us," Morrie nudged me in the arm. I couldn't look, obviously, but I could listen, and a distinctive voice carried through the wall.

"...excellent take for the first day of the festival, Lawerence. This little scheme of mine will prove to be our most lucrative yet. I knew it was time to get out of London – these country bumpkins will lap up any little bit of culture they can get."

Mr. Rasmussen. Our sworn enemy.

And from what he was saying, he was *up to something.*

"...I mean, just *look* at this event," Mr. Rasmussen continued, loud enough for all of us to hear. "Certainly, the pop-up theater is an interesting idea, but it's ruined by the amateur acting and the carnival antics and the complete lack of class and good taste. The woman running the festival wouldn't know culture if it fell out of a tree and smacked her in her straw bonnet."

"That's it. No one insults our village or Mrs. Ellis, except me." Heathcliff balled his hands into fists. "Want me to go over there and get all Shylock on him, bring back a pound of posh wanker flesh?"

"Take my sword." Morrie held it out. "It's nice and sharp. If you get a clean cut, we can turn his skin into throw pillows."

The voices dropped to a whisper. I guess they heard us.

Serves him right. I hope he can't sleep tonight for worrying about the *country bumpkins* coming to skin him alive.

"I could fly over there," Quoth murmured. "I could eavesdrop on what they're talking about."

"No need." I settled back into my chair, patting Oscar's collar as I pressed my ear to the thin plywood that formed the wall between our boxes. "I got this."

It was a common misconception that people who were blind had heightened senses. You didn't lose your sight and suddenly become Daredevil, but you *did* learn to use your other senses in a different way. I'd become quite good at picking out individual sounds from a cacophony of noise, which means I was easily able to eavesdrop on Mr. Rasmussen's conversation over the hum of the busy theater.

"...don't you worry," Rasmussen was saying. "This isn't exactly a village of scholars and gentlemen. You saw that dusty old hovel they call a bookshop. We're perfectly safe here."

Safe? What does he mean by safe?

"I just know I'd feel better if we pulled the book off public display," Lawrence Delacroix said. "Surely, we don't need to bring all this attention down on our heads? Jasper, you know I only say this because of how I feel about—"

"Not now, Lawrence," Mr. Rasmussen cut him off, his voice curt and uncaring. "The ceremony is starting."

And it was. The light shifted, dimming in the galleries until we sat in darkness. Visible through the open roof, stars glittered across a midnight blanket. Luckily, the British weather was playing fair tonight, and there wasn't a cloud in the sky.

I gasped as haunting music stirred, and feet clopped across the stage. Although I couldn't see them, I'd seen enough rehearsals to know three black-clad figures had crowded around a cauldron, which slowly glowed with bright orange flames to appreciative 'ooohs' and 'aaahs' from the audience.

Quoth had been working on the cauldron yesterday, rigging the orange LED lights inside it to cast an eerie, flickering glow over the faces of Mrs. Ellis, Cynthia Lachlan, and my mother, who wore hooked noses and had their faces decorated with boils. From our view above the stage, all I could make out was the shimmering orange circle of the cauldron with shadowy hands moving over it. The effect sent a delicious chill down my spine.

"Double, double toil and trouble;" my mother cooed. "Fire burn and cauldron bubble."

"Fillet of a fenny snake, In the cauldron boil and bake;" Mrs. Ellis cackled. "Eye of newt and toe of frog, Wool of bat and tongue of dog…"

Morrie's breath kissed my ear. "Macbeth."

"Shut up."

As the witches cast their spell, the house lights slowly went up and the band kicked off a jaunty tune. To whoops and hollers from the audience, the three Weird Sisters raced to the front of the stage, threw off their black cloaks to reveal sparkly red underthings, and did a sexy hiphop dance to Creedence Clearwater Revival's "Bad Moon Rising." Being that my mother was down there being wolf-whistled at, I was glad all I could make out was the black circumference of her witch's hat. Being blind had its benefits.

When the Weird Sisters finished their number, they danced offstage to riotous applause, and another figure entered. It was Miles Stapleton, resplendent in his gold-brocaded robe. When the applause died down, he spoke into the microphone.

"Thank you for supporting the Argleton Shakespeare Festival and the inaugural season of the New New Globe Theater. We have an exciting program of events for you over the next three weeks, including daily performances of three of Shakespeare's most beloved plays on a rotating basis, *Macbeth, A Midsummer Night's Dream*, and *Romeo and Juliet*. We're also hosting a lecture series from our own world-renowned Shakespeare scholar, a Shakespearean-themed menu and quiz night at the Rose & Wimple, a fairy grotto for the children, *and* we even have our very own First Folio on display in the village. That's right – it's quite a coup. For your own look at this wonder, visit Rasmussen's Books – the official bookshop of the festival – in the village green, and head to his booth in the beer garden after the show to get your Bard merchandise."

I ground my teeth together. Morrie squeezed my thigh.

"Patience, gorgeous. We won't allow this fiend to ruin your festival."

Puck popped his head up between us. "I could anoint his eyes, and transform him into—"

"No." Heathcliff, Quoth, and I said together.

I turned my attention back to the stage. Miles had moved toward the edge, his voice booming. "Tonight, we've put together a little showcase of all the festival has to offer – a highlight reel if you will, of scenes from all three plays. But first, let us place the Bard in context, and learn a little about his life. Without further ado, I'd like to welcome Argleton's very own Barded-Lady, haha, Zenzile Monroe."

We clapped as the stage crew brought out two chairs, and Zen swept onstage in her Lady Macbeth costume. She took a deep bow and allowed Miles to escort her to her seat. In the Lord's Room next to mine, I heard Rasmussen hiss under his breath.

"Now, Zen, I hardly think you need an introduction," Miles said. "You're the director of our beloved Shakespeare Museum, and one of my historical consultants for the construction of the New New Globe. Many people in the audience tonight remember Shakespeare as that boring bloke from English class at school who said all the funny words. They might feel like a festival celebrating his work is not for them. Could you tell them why they're going to love what we put together?"

"Thank you, Miles. Yes, I can. Contrary to what *some people* think," Zen's words sliced the air like a knife, "Shakespeare should be enjoyed by everyone. It's a complete myth that you have to be some kind of English scholar to understand him."

I heard a derisive snort from the box next to ours.

Zen continued. "Shakespeare wrote for the masses, the common people, those with the penny seats right down the front." A roar went up from the floor, and for a moment I kind of wished I was down there, too. "That's why I think it's so appalling that his First Folio will go into the hands of a private collector, and not to the museum where everyone could enjoy it." She paused. "It makes me so angry I could *murder*."

"Murder, of course, is a key theme in many of Shakespeare's plays. Can you talk to this…"

Zen and Miles covered all kinds of interesting facts in their talk, and when they were done, the actors from Romeo and Juliet came out to perform a raucous fight scene, running through the groundlings and even into our private box in their enthusiasm. I laughed and clapped along with everyone, but all the while, Zen's words nagged in the back of my mind.

I detested Rasmussen as much as she did, and his attitude that books should be locked away for only the elite made me sick, but the way she said the word murder…

…it was as if she truly meant it.

CHAPTER EIGHT

*D*uring the intermission, we went down to the beer
garden, where the Weird Sisters were holding court.

"Mum, you were fantastic." I gave her a big hug. Behind her,
her boyfriend, Handy Andy, couldn't stop beaming as he held
Mum's arm possessively and pinched her bum.

"Oooh, you ratbag." Mum slapped him playfully.

I squeezed Oscar's lead, not sure how I felt about my mum's
PDA with Andy, especially after I heard the love in my father's
voice and I knew he still thought of her. But he was the time-
traveling poet Homer and she was a middle-aged tarot reader
who raised me all on her own, so she deserved a guy who made
her happy. "And the costume fits okay?"

"Mina, it's perfect." Mum smoothed her hands over the red
sequins, shimmying her ass in a way that made me feel vaguely
queasy. "You have a real talent. I'm so happy you're still able to
enjoy fashion."

"Me too." I smiled. "I'm hoping that if the festival goes well
and the New New Globe goes on tour, Miles might ask me to
come along and help with wardrobe—"

I was cut off by Andy and Mum sharing a loud, slurpy kiss.

Morrie – sensing I needed rescuing – barged his way into our group, with Puck trailing behind him.

"Hello, Mrs. Wilde. It's a pleasure to see you both again." Morrie winked at Puck. "I'm so looking forward to our scenes together in Macbeth."

"Argh!" Puck tore at his hair and started doing his crazy jig again.

"Whatever is he doing?" Mum frowned at Puck.

"It's an old theater superstition," Morrie explained. "He has to do that every time I say 'Macbeth'—"

"Please desist," Puck cried as he spun faster, his hands flailing wildly.

"What was that?" Morrie asked sweetly. "You want me to stop saying 'Macbeth'?"

"Aaaaargh!"

Puck half ran, half jigged out of the theater. Morrie and I collapsed into giggles.

"I was looking for you, gorgeous." Morrie placed a glass in my hand. "I've got you a cocktail. It's called the Taming of the Shrewdriver."

"You're my hero." I accepted the glass, and Morrie slipped his arm into mine, leading me away from Mum and Andy, who didn't even seem to notice we disappeared.

"I vote we skip out on the second half," Morrie bent his head to whisper delicious words against my ear. "I want to get you back to Nevermore so I can undo those corset laces with such excruciating leisure that you beg me to fuck you – because you, Mina Wilde, in this outfit, are my fucking fantasy."

At his filthy words, a shiver of anticipation flushed over my skin. I went to get Heathcliff and Quoth and rush back to Nevermore, but Morrie stopped me.

"First, I think there's something you should see."

He led me and Oscar across the beer garden to a group of people crowded around a table. I fumed because I knew exactly what that table was – not a week before, Mrs. Ellis showed me that space and told me that was where Nevermore Bookshop would set up. But instead, it was Mr. Rasmussen with his chest puffed out and his imperious attitude hogging all our customers.

"You might not be able to see," Morrie whispered, "but he has no books for sale."

What?

No books?

"But he's the official festival bookseller," I said. "The whole *point* of the official bookseller is to show up at all the events with books for the public to buy. That's why our storage room is filled with Shakespearean tomes and Zen's scholarly volumes. What's he doing—"

"It's very disappointing," Cynthia Lachlan said as she walked past. "I wanted to buy a playbook for my daughter, but all that guy is doing is giving out these."

She thrust a paper into my hands. I passed it to Morrie, and he read it aloud. It was a pamphlet directing people to visit Rasmussen books to see the First Folio and the other treasures in their collection for a fee. And 'serious inquiries only' could come for a private viewing to discuss a price for the books. Gross.

All around me, I heard disappointed people who wanted to buy books but couldn't. These were my people, my customers, and I hated that they were missing out on this opportunity to immerse themselves in Shakespeare because Rasmussen was a snob.

"Mrs. Ellis," I called out. She appeared by my side in a flash, her director's clipboard in her hands. "Mr. Rasmussen doesn't have any books for sale."

"Oh, yes," she frowned at the table. "He said he couldn't get stock in time, so he's promoting the First Folio instead."

"They gave the bookseller position to a guy who seems determined not to sell books, who hates on the citizens of this village, instead of to Mina, who has always supported all the kooky things in this village," Heathcliff's boomed as he joined us, his voice taking on a quality that suggested he was about to get stabby.

"It's okay, Heathcliff," I said. "It's not important who runs the stall. What's important is that people have the best time at the Shakespeare Festival, and that includes buying the books they want to read. Rasmussen has no stock, and we're got a storage room filled with books we can't sell. Tomorrow, we're going to head over to Rasmussen's before he opens, and we'll talk to him civilly about how we can work together to make the festival a success."

"Oh, Mina, that would be wonderful." Mrs. Ellis pecked my cheek. "It would be a load off my mind not to hear people complaining that they couldn't get books."

"So no stabbing?" Heathcliff sounded disappointed.

"No stabbing." I jabbed my finger into Puck's chest. "And you're not turning him into a donkey, either."

"What about a fox?" Puck asked. "Thou could wear him as a stole?"

"No turning people into animals. Or potted plants. Or tug boats," I growled. "We are going to solve this like adults. Now, make yourself scarce for the evening because I'm going home so my boyfriends can shag my brains out."

CHAPTER NINE

*M*y alarm rang, startling me out of dreams of Heathcliff in pantaloons. (If you want my personal opinion, all men look better in pantaloons.) I rolled over and hit the button that read out the time in a tinny AI voice.

6:45AM.

Why the fuck is the alarm set for 6:45?

Is this one of Morrie's pranks?

I reached across to shut the bloody thing off, then remembered with a start that *I* was the architect of my own demise. I was the one who set it at this ungodly hour. We were going to talk to Mr. Rasmussen. After three Taming of the Shrewdrivers and the mind-blowing sex last night, it completely slipped my mind.

Now I was awake, my mind whirring. I had so many ideas about how our two bookshops could work together to make this the best Shakespeare festival ever.

This was my chance to shine as Mina the business person. Rasmussen Books was going to be around a lot longer than the festival, and Mr. Rasmussen was right in saying our stores catered to different clientele. We could complement each other instead of competing.

Do you really want to work with that guy? The niggling voice inside my head reminded me of what I overheard last night in the Lord's Rooms. Rasmussen and his apprentice sounded like they were up to something fishy, and if that was true, I didn't want Nevermore caught up in it.

But there's no harm in going to talk to him. We're not asking him to rob a bank with us, but if we could offload our books, it would sure help pay this month's bills.

I sat up and felt over the sheets. Heathcliff was still in bed, one enormous arm draped protectively across my chest. Both Morrie and Quoth were already up. That didn't surprise me. Quoth often rose with the sun – he was probably painting in his attic studio. And Morrie was probably tending to the morning coffee run. My criminal mastermind liked to beat the crowds to Oliver's so he got first choice of the scones.

"Get up." I nudged the slumbering bear beside me.

"No," came the surly reply from somewhere in the blankets. "I want to stay here, where there are no customers or crazy girl-friends who force me to wear ruffles."

"We're going to talk to Rasmussen. Up. Up. Up." I whomped him over the head with the pillow. Morrie poked his head in the door, bearing cups of steaming coffee.

"Oh, pillow fight. I want to play." He set down the cups and reached across the bed to grab me.

"I wasn't—" But my protests were smothered by Morrie's lips, hot and possessive and utterly in control. He kissed me so hard that I sank into him, my grip relaxing. When James Moriarty commanded with his lips and his hands and his body, I surrendered utterly.

Before I knew it, he whipped the pillow from my hand and thumped me across the back.

"Oof. Oh, no you don't. That's war." I yanked the other pillow from under Heathcliff's head and whomped Morrie with it. Feathers flew everywhere. Morrie swung again, but I flattened myself against the bed and he missed. I caught him on the backswing, sending him reeling. He cried out with surprise.

"You want to play rough, gorgeous?" A cruel smile twisted across Morrie's lips as he grabbed the edge of the duvet, ready to tear it from around our naked bodies.

"No games. She's mine." Heathcliff grabbed me around the waist and yanked me so that my back pressed against his hard chest. He bent his head over my shoulder to claim my mouth in a rough kiss while his hands roamed down the front of my sleepshirt, popping open the buttons one by one. His fingers rolled my nipple until it hardened into a sensitive ball, which Heathcliff toyed with in that feral way of his until I gasped against his kiss.

"And you're both *mine.*" Morrie dropped the duvet and crawled onto the bed. He grabbed Heathcliff by the throat and tilted his head, devouring him like he was a juicy steak and Morrie hadn't eaten in days.

Morrie and Heathcliff as an item was still new to me, but sharing them with each other when they were this hot was no trouble at all.

The pair of them turned to me with hunger in their eyes, and my insides melted into a puddle. Morrie pressed himself against me, sandwiching me between his wiry frame and Heathcliff's sturdy barrel chest.

"We don't have time for this," I breathed.

"Then we'd better make it quick," Morrie smirked. "What do you say, Lord Grumperton? Want to break a record for the number of times we can make Mina come in under ten minutes?"

"Challenge accepted," Heathcliff growled against my ear.

Morrie spun me around so that my chest pressed to Heathcliff. This close, my gothic antihero stole my breath away. His dark, anthracite orbs fixed on me with unblemished tenderness, a

71

look that Emily Brontë would have us believe the cruel and twisted Heathcliff incapable of gifting.

Heathcliff must've read my thoughts on my face. He chuckled darkly, the rumble of it vibrating against my skin.

I wrapped my legs around him and he sheathed himself inside me with a sigh, his shoulders relaxing as he crushed our bodies together, as we became as close in body and spirit as two people can be. Even like this, raw and tender and quiet, Heathcliff's strength made him something to behold. Loving him was like loving the bitter cold of winter on your skin, or a storm of dark clouds raging across the moors.

Loving him meant being swept away in his wildness.

Our bodies moved together, his cock stretching me, reaching and rubbing against all the places that felt so good. A coil of tension wound inside me, a bowstring being drawn tight. I bucked my hips to meet each of Heathcliff's deep, long thrusts, winding and winding that string tight.

Heathcliff had so enraptured me that I didn't even notice Morrie fussing with a bottle of lube until he bent over, his lean body folding around me. He slid a lubed-up finger around to the front between me and Heathcliff, and circled it over my clit. I gritted my teeth, not wanting to give the Napoleon of Crime the satisfaction of seeing me come so quickly, but Heathcliff made a little sigh against my mouth and I was gone.

The bowstring snapped, unfurling inside me in waves of melting pleasure. I sank into Morrie, my lips falling from Heathcliff's mouth as my body surrendered to the sensation.

"One," Morrie whispered in my ear. He refused to let up, his finger turning languid circles on my clit as Heathcliff thrust inside me. I wriggled my hips, trying to escape the onslaught of Morrie's finger, but he wouldn't let me. He liked the game, and now I was caught in his snare, he didn't intend to let me go.

Even though a sliver of pain chased the pleasure that still pulsed in my veins, I rose to meet it, squeezing my thighs to draw

Heathcliff even deeper. He bent down and dragged his teeth over my nipple, and I was gone again. Shock waves rocked my body as another orgasm claimed me.

"Two," Morrie whispered. "Are you ready for me now, gorgeous?"

My skin was on fire. My facial muscles didn't work. The only thing I could do was moan, "Yeeeeeee…"

Heathcliff gathered me in his strong arms, holding me close while Morrie lined up the head of his cock at my rear entrance. As Morrie pushed inside, I cried out against Heathcliff's lips. We'd done this a few times now, with two of them inside me at once, and every time it felt…like *perfection*. Like heaven. Like complete surrender.

"Don't forget to breathe, gorgeous." Morrie chuckled, his voice dark and tinged with lust.

Heathcliff held me still, his cock twitching as Morrie pushed inside, a little at a time, the lube easing his way as his head slid past the tight ring of muscle. I focused on breathing in Heathcliff's wild, peaty scent as the two of them stretched me right to the edge of pain.

With a final thrust, Morrie seated himself deep inside me. He leaned over my shoulder to claim Heathcliff's mouth as his own. With the pair of them being so…well, so *Morrie* and *Heathcliff,* sex was usually a battle of wills, but this felt different. Heathcliff let out with a contented sigh as he cupped Morrie's cheek in his huge hand. He drew back a little so Morrie could drive deep, not letting me stop for a breath until he was deeper inside me than I ever thought possible.

Morrie rocked back and Heathcliff thrust forward, their lengths drawing along each other through the thin wall inside me. Heathcliff growled low in his throat as he fucked Morrie's mouth with his tongue. This wasn't just about the two of them pleasuring me – although there was definitely plenty of that going on, let me tell you – but they were surrendering to each other.

They built a rhythm between them, rocking back and forth inside me. I could not describe how intense it felt, how intimate and perfect and spellbinding it was to be taken by them, possessed by them, loved by them both. All the while, Morrie's finger drummed a relentless rhythm against my clit, drawing me back into myself until the whole world narrowed to the red dot in the center of my vision.

I floated outside of my body, only drawn back when Morrie's breath tickled my ear.

"Three."

As another growl tore from his throat, Heathcliff leaned forward. He shoved Morrie's shoulder to push him back on the bed. Morrie's teeth dug into my skin as Heathcliff bore down on us. He pinned us both, trapping us with his weight and his dark, possessive gaze. With all the passion in his dark, feral heart, Heathcliff slammed us into the bed. The brass bedstead crashed against the wall as he fucked both of us at the same time. It was hot and needy and so so spellbinding Morrie gasped beneath me, and I felt his cock tighten inside me, and even though I didn't think I had anything left, another orgasm grabbed me and tossed me about like a ship lost at sea during a tempest.

I don't know how long I rode the wave, floating in an ocean of pure pleasure, but when I came back to earth again, Heathcliff pulled back and he stared down at me, his untamed curls stuck with downy feathers.

"Four," Heathcliff sounded amazed.

"No fair," I managed to choke out. "That last one was stolen."

"Can't steal from the willing." Morrie grinned. He slid out from beneath me and wrapped a towel around himself. Feathers stuck to his back. "If anyone wants me, I'll be in the shower, making myself presentable for the great Rasmussen. He looks like the sort of fellow who really needs a good fucking."

"Shit." I forced my limbs to move. It took a few tries, but I rolled over and grabbed my phone. I pressed the button that made it read out the time. "We're late."

I scrambled out of bed. The sheets tangled around me and I went flying. Two warm arms slid around me, holding me up so I didn't fall. *Quoth.* Always Quoth keeping me together. Keeping our messy little family together.

"It looks like you've massacred some of my friends," he said, smiling at the little downy feathers littering every surface.

"I got Morrie in the face, so they died for a good cause." I sagged against Quoth. Four orgasms in under ten minutes meant my legs didn't work properly. "We're going to have to hurry. Morrie's in the shower, so that will take seven centuries, and I have to deal with Oscar and get caffeine—"

"I've taken Oscar for his walk. And I got the coffee." He pressed my reusable cup into my hand. Quoth found it for me online – it was toughened glass and had little raised dog paw prints around the rim.

I took a deep sip of coffee. Some of Oliver's best work. "Thank you. I have caffeine in my veins. I can do this."

I hunted through my clothes to find my best 'businesstime Mina' outfit (black vintage velvet blazer, skinny black slacks, black velvet ballet flats, and Clash tee, in case you were wondering), pulled my hair back into a messy bun, and hammered on the bathroom door until Morrie emerged in a cloud of aftershave and perfection. He was wearing the suit I saw him in the day we met, the one with exquisite tailoring and pleats so sharp they could cut skin. He rubbed his hands together with glee.

"No," I wiggled my finger at him.

"No what?" His voice was the definition of innocent.

"No to whatever scheme you're concocting."

Quoth transformed into his raven and perched on my shoulder. Unlike Morrie, he didn't like confrontation of any sort, and he felt safer as a raven.

Heathcliff emerged from the kitchen, his morning whisky in his hand. He'd put on a dark shirt rolled up to the elbows so everyone could see his bulging forearms and the tattoos winding over his dark skin. He was our muscle. If I couldn't persuade Rasmussen with niceness, then Heathcliff could do it with menace.

I picked up Oscar's harness, and he practically pulled me down the stairs, he was so excited to go out again. Oscar loved working as my guide dog, and he was still young and full of energy, which made him the perfect dog for my hectic life.

"I want to join." Puck came racing out of the Children's room, where he'd been sleeping on the fold-out. Usually, we tried to find jobs for fictional characters. Lydia Bennet was currently breaking hearts in officer training for Her Majesty's Navy. Socrates was a social media star appearing on morning telly shows opposite his hero, the modern philosopher Peter Jordanson.

But Puck…what could we do with a fairy that turned people into donkeys just to amuse himself? We tried getting him a job at the local petting zoo, but he gave the lion two heads and turned a zookeeper into a penguin. He was staying at the shop until we could figure out what to do with him.

Maybe Rasmussen would take on a mischievous fae who leaves a trail of chaos and mayhem in his wake?

I sighed. "Okay, but no donkeys."

Puck clasped his hand to his breast. "Upon my heart, no donkeys."

The five of us set out from the bookshop. The crisp morning air caressed my skin, and I cursed myself for not putting a thermal vest on. Businesstime Mina apparently didn't dress for the dreary British weather.

As we rounded the end of Butcher Street in front of Oliver's bakery, Oscar drew up short, stopping me in my tracks just as an American voice said, "Whoa there, Nelly."

"Hello, Mr. Abernathy." I'd recognize that Southern accent anywhere. "I'm sorry for startling you. We didn't see you there."

"Quite all right, young lady." Mr. Abernathy's voice was muffled. I realized I couldn't see his face over the huge bakery box in his arms. It looked like he cleaned Oliver out. "I was just out for a spot of delicious British baking, and I thought I'd try and catch Mr. Rasmussen before he opened his store."

"That's funny. We were actually hoping to talk to him ourselves."

"I wouldn't bother. That man is dead to the world. I hammered on that door like a stallion among the fillies, and no one answered. Say, this town may not have a decent fried chicken establishment, but this bakery ain't half bad. I've been acquainting myself with your hot meat pies." He lowered the box and pointed to his chest. "Acquainting myself all over."

He has an enormous sauce stain on his shirt, Quoth whispered inside my head.

"You should try Oliver's scones," I said. "With jam and clotted cream. They're to die for. Were you going to talk to Rasmussen about the First Folio?"

Hiram shook his head angrily. "He should know not to piss on my leg and tell me it's raining. He promised that book to me. We may not have had anything in writing, but it was a gentleman's agreement. I even offered him a substantial cash bonus to take the Folio off his hands immediately, but he ain't budging and my wife has joined me for the festival and…"

Hiram cast a worried look across the green, in the direction of the Rose Cottage, the nicest B&B in the village.

Something about what Hiram Abernathy said struck me as odd. Would a man like Rasmussen really turn down the chance to sell a rare book for a lot of extra money just to display it in a tiny Shakespeare festival in a village he didn't even seem to like very much? He'd have to sell a lot of admission tickets to make up the difference. And I doubted anyone else would step forward with an offer with as deep pockets as Hiram Abernathy.

But then I remembered how proud Shelley was of her dad when I spoke to her yesterday. Maybe he was trying to do something nice for the village to show his daughter that he wanted to improve their relationship. Maybe Jasper Rasmussen had a heart after all—

"Hiram Abernathy, you best not be out there eating those sugary pastries, or you are as dead as a doornail."

"Oh, no," Hiram ducked behind a park bench, clutching his package close to his chest. His voice trembled with fear. "Hide me."

"Hiram," the voice screeched. It appeared to be coming closer. "I've made your kale and beet smoothie. If you don't show yourself *this minute*—"

"Looks like your goose is cooked, mate," Heathcliff said in a completely serious voice. Behind me, Morrie snorted with laughter. Hiram flattened himself against the grass, but it was no good, he was completely obvious.

"Hiram Abernathy, what are you doing—"

Puck raised a finger. The air sizzled with sparkling energy. My ears popped.

When I looked down at the park bench, instead of an oil baron cowering with his contraband pastries, all I saw was a pile of crumpled clothing and a fuzzy, rather confused-looking donkey.

CHAPTER TEN

"*H*eehaw?" said Hiram Abernathy.

"Puck!" I yelled.

"What?" the fairy grinned. "Thou sayeth no donkeys, but since he is an ass, I hath made him so."

I turned to Morrie, who said with a chuckle, "Technically, Puck's correct. He's turned Abernathy into a *kulan*, which is a variety of Asiatic ass, and a different species from a donkey—"

"Hee-haw." The donkey nudged one of the fallen bakery boxes. It was still wearing Abernathy's Stetson, and as it bowed its head, the hat slid over one of its huge, brown eyes.

I grabbed for the donkey's mane and glared at Puck. "Speaking of asses, stop being a smartass and change him back."

"But I jest to make you smile." Puck's smile broadened. "And you are but smiling."

It was true, dammit. Hiram looked so ridiculous as a donkey, with his big white hat, and he did ask us to hide him. But what he was hiding from—

"Why, hello there, you lovely young things," a Southern voice drawled. A woman wearing a bright yellow sundress and white cowboy boots stalked up to us. She carried a cup containing something that looked like orange snot, and bore the smile of a tiger about to pounce. "Have y'all seen my husband, Hiram Abernathy? He snuck out of our hotel room while my back was turned, without taking his morning smoothie. He's a big fella, wearing a Stetson and a guilty-as-sin look on his face—"

Morrie surreptitiously plucked the Stetson from the donkey's head and dropped it in the rubbish bin. "We're sorry, we haven't seen anyone like that."

The donkey nodded its head vigorously as it kicked Hiram's clothing under the bench.

The woman narrowed her eyes at the donkey. "Why are y'all walking a donkey around the village? With a dog in a coat and a crow, I might add. You some kind of circus act?"

Did she just call me a crow? Quoth hopped up and down on my shoulder. *She'd better watch out, or I'll give her a little flavoring for her smoothie—*

"He's a raven, actually." I patted Quoth's head. "And this is Oscar, my guide dog. As for the donkey, well…he's an actor in the Shakespeare Festival. I'm Mina Wilde. I run a bookstore in the village. And you must be Hiram's wife." I held out my hand to her. "Happy birthday."

"Thank you, my dear. I'm Dolores Abernathy, delighted to meet you." She gave my hand a firm shake. "Yes, it is my birthday, which is why I'm fit to be tied that Hiram's disappeared on me. I left my precious ranch behind to join him in this godforsaken country because he promised me something special, but now that he's run away, I suspect he was lying like a dog on a rug. When I get my hands on him, why I'll…" She mimed wringing someone's neck.

"*Heeeeeeeeeeehaw!*" Hiram reared up on his hind legs and took off across the green, nearly bowling over Miles Stapleton, who'd just stepped out from the alley behind the shops. Miles yelled as he dropped his briefcase, but Hiram didn't stop. The donkey (sorry, ass) warbled as he barreled toward the pub.

"Oi, watch it." Richard was serving breakfast on the outdoor tables. He leaped out of the way, spilling a Full English on Hiram's face as he took cover behind a planter box. "Someone get control of that mule!"

"Technically, he's an ass," Morrie yelled merrily.

"I'll help you." Dolores stalked toward the pub. "I've broken in many an unruly horse in my time, and this creature's no different. You need a firm hand and a sharp spur and—"

"Heeeeeehaw." A terrified Hiram bowled over several tables and disappeared down the road toward the church, with Dolores swaggering after him.

"It looks like Hiram's felt the sting of her firm hand one too many times," Morrie laughed. I hid my grin behind my hand. I couldn't help it – Hiram the ass did look pretty funny bolting down the road to get away from his wife. And he left all his illicit snacks behind. I picked up one of the bakery boxes and pulled out an untouched chocolate doughnut.

"Let's get out of here before someone blames us for this mess." I glared at Puck. "And *change him back.*"

"Those things do best please thee, that befell preposterously," Puck pouted, but he waved his finger again, and I heard the sizzle and pop of his magic shifting in the air.

"Good, thank you. Now, can we get to the bookshop without further incidents—"

Morrie yelled and threw a hand in front of me, but not before I turned on my heel and slammed into someone coming the other way.

"Arf," Oscar barked, as if admonishing me that I was supposed to wait for him to lead the way.

"I'm so sorry. It happens sometimes. I didn't see you." My face flushed with embarrassment as I untangled myself from the poor unfortunate who'd been in the path of a blind girl on a mission. "Do you want some doughnuts as an apology? The donkey didn't tread on them—Oh, hello, Zen."

"H-hello Mina." Zen looked startled as she brushed herself off. "It's quite all right, not your fault at all. I was just out on my morning run and I wasn't looking where I was going."

"Are you okay? You seem a little out of sorts?" And I couldn't help but notice she was wearing a nice blouse and trousers, not running clothes.

"I'm fine. I just…" Zen wrung her hands. "I was just…um, well, I don't know what I was doing, actually. I came to make another fruitless attempt to convince Jasper Rasmussen to donate the Folio to the museum, but he's not in his shop."

"We heard. Hiram Abernathy was looking for him, too. Maybe he's late to work today. It must take him a lot of time in the morning to polish his devil horns."

Heathcliff snorted, but Zen didn't seem to hear my joke. "Listen, Mina, it's lovely to see you, but I think I…I need to get home. And have my shower. Yes, and my vitamins. I'll see you tonight for our first performance, Morrie—"

Zen was interrupted by a commotion on the edge of the green as a figure barreled into Richard, splattering eggs, hash browns, sausages, and black pudding in all directions. The figure didn't stop, but kept on flying toward us.

"Out of my way," Shelley Rasmussen barked, shoving Max's stroller so hard that it slammed into Heathcliff's legs.

"Shelley, stop that. Are you okay?"

"No, I'm bloody not okay, am I?" she snapped as she swerved around us. "I thought my father came to the village to spend time with us, but it was just another one of his lies. I'm going home, and I'm not going to bother with him and his nonsense ever again."

"Can you tell us what happened? Have you seen your father this morning?" I called out, but no one replied.

"She's gone," Heathcliff said. "Unlike the bruise on my shins."

"It sounds like everyone's got it in for Mr. Rasmussen today," I said. "Maybe this will make him change his tune."

"It also sounds like he's not opening the door to anyone," Heathcliff tugged my arm back toward Nevermore. "So we could go back to bed and Morrie could rub arnica cream on my bruised shin—"

"Rasmussen will open the door to us," I said. "He can't say no to a business opportunity. And if he doesn't, we've got Puck."

Puck bowed deeply. "At your service, My Queen."

"You don't have to bow," I said. "Although I like this 'My Queen' business; you can keep that up."

As a group, we walked across the square to the darkened entrance of Mr. Rasmussen's shop. Beside the door was the table he was using to take tickets. The sign said he opened in twenty-five minutes, and it wouldn't be long until the first busload of tourists arrived in the village and people started lining up. *He has to be inside.*

I knocked on the door. No answer. The front windows were in shadow, but when I cupped my hands on the glass, I thought I could see a faint light in the back of the shop.

Morrie tried the handle. "That's odd. It's unlocked."

He pushed the door open, and we crowded inside. I saw I was right – the lights behind the counter at the back were on, and the display cases glowed, but the main shop lights were still off so I could barely see a thing. Morrie fumbled around and found the light switches, but the place was so dark they barely made a difference.

Narrow glass display cases ran down the length of the room, acting like a funnel directing foot traffic to the far end, where an elaborate counter and viewing area with velvet cradles and all kinds of magnifying glasses were set out. Morrie went into the back storage room while Heathcliff loomed in the doorway. Quoth fluttered around, peering up a narrow flight of stairs roped off with a NO CUSTOMERS sign.

"Mr. Rasmussen," I yelled. "It's Mina Wilde from Nevermore

Bookshop. I came to talk to you about the festival bookshop. I have a proposal that would be in your best interests to—"

"Uh, Mina," Morrie called from behind the counter, his voice uncharacteristically serious. "I don't think we'll be working with Mr. Rasmussen."

"Don't be ridiculous. He's a businessman. He's not going to turn away from a business relationship no matter how much he turns his giant nose up at us."

"No, that's not what I mean." Morrie stepped aside, giving me a view of a dark lump on the floor. "He's dead."

CHAPTER ELEVEN

"Oh, no, not again." I shuffled between the narrow shelves to reach Morrie. Wordlessly, he swung the desk lamp down so I could make out the shape of Rasmussen's body on the floor. He'd collapsed on his chest, his legs tangled around the leg of his chair that had toppled over beside him. His immaculate suit was all scrunched up, and a dark pool of blood widened around his head.

Oscar stuck his nose out to have a sniff, and I pulled him back.

"Yes. Again." Heathcliff loomed over my shoulder, his breath tickling my earlobe. "He's shut up shop, taken a permanent vacation, turned in his Tesco clubcard, liquidated his stock, and checked into the horizontal Hilton—"

"He's shuffled off this mortal coil," Morrie put in. "Hamlet said that."

"Stop. It's not funny. A man is dead." I didn't like Mr. Rasmussen, but that didn't mean I wanted him to *die*.

"He was a wanker," Heathcliff said. "It's a little funny. How did he die, anyway? Heart attack from looking at Dan Brown's sales numbers?"

Impaled himself on his own nose? Quoth added. *Sorry, I couldn't resist.*

"Well, I'm no Jo, but it looks like he fell over and hit his head on the side of the desk." Morrie bent down to inspect the body. He pointed to something on the corner of the desk, beneath a pot containing some kind of flower. "He has a rather nasty wound on the side of his head...actually, I think there are two wounds, one much worse than the other. And I see a few splatters of blood on this cabinet, so maybe an accident..."

"This was no accident," Heathcliff said. "Look."

He pointed to a velvet cradle on the end of the counter. I was surprised I hadn't noticed it already, as it held pride of place on top of a satin-covered plinth. The attached sign read, 'Shakespeare's First Folio,' in letters large enough even I could read them.

Only the cradle was empty.

The First Folio was gone.

CHAPTER TWELVE

*S*omeone killed Mr. Rasmussen and stole the First Folio.

"We have to call the police." I backed away from the scene. "We need to get out of here and not touch anything. This must be a robbery gone wrong. The thieves had a copy of Rasmussen's key, or came in through the back, and they didn't expect him to be here so early and they—"

"This cannot be a robbery." Puck picked something off the ground and held it out to me. "The book thou seekest is right here."

"What are you doing?" I shoved Puck's arm away. He dropped the book in fright. "Your fingerprints are now all over that book, which means the police might think you had something to do with this murder. You're already going to be in trouble for turning Hiram Abernathy into an ass, and now you've tampered with a crime scene."

Puck held up his hands. "Forgive me, Queen of Nevermore, I mistook—"

"None of your nonsense, fairy. We need to *think*. Mina, look at this." Morrie had already pulled on a pair of immaculate white gloves, which he kept in his pockets at all times because that was the kind of guy Morrie was. He moved the book under another lamp and flicked it on, pointing to an area of the cover. In the beam of light I could make out a dark stain in the corner, across the pages.

"Is that…"

"In my professional opinion, that's blood," Morrie said. "And, again, I'm no Jo, but I believe the corner of this book perfectly matches the wound in the side of Rasmussen's head. This wasn't a robbery gone wrong. Old Rasmussen here was clobbered over the head with his own First Folio."

CHAPTER THIRTEEN

I stared down at the book that had caused so much drama in the village. It was large, about twelve inches high, eight inches wide, with a spine of about two inches in thickness encased in a heavy goatskin binding. If swung with enough force, it could definitely cause damage. And if Mr. Rasmussen was taken by surprise and fell back and hit his head on the edge of his desk… it would explain the two wounds Morrie saw…

Another murder in Argleton.

Right under my nose.

At least this time, it looks to be a purely human affair – nothing supernatural involved.

One thing was certain – whoever did this knew our unfortunate bookseller. The front door was unlocked. There were two empty coffee cups on the desk and a small plate of fancy shortbread biscuits. Mr. Rasmussen had turned up to the shop early, expecting a guest. Only instead of a business meeting, he got bumped off with his own prized book.

Unless… I guessed it was possible that the killer came in the back way and then unlocked and left by the front door, but that was unlikely because we saw Shelley and Hiram and Zen on the green, all wanting to talk to Mr. Rasmussen, and one of them would've seen someone leave by the front door.

Unless one of them was the killer.

They were all in the vicinity of Rasmussen's shop. Both Zen and Hiram were angry enough about how Rasmussen was conducting himself over the First Folio that they could've snapped. Shelley wouldn't kill her own father, surely? But she *was* agitated this morning, and running in the opposite direction of the shop…

But we don't know when this murder occurred. He could've been lying here for hours. Don't jump to conclusions, Mina. There are a lot of people in this village who had a reason to hate Mr. Rasmussen.

Our immediate problem was that the police wouldn't look at them if they got distracted by Puck's fingerprints…

"Puck," I hissed. "You swear you didn't do this?"

"Upon my heart," he clasped his hand over his chest.

"Then make like a bird and get the flock out of here. If anyone asks, you were never here with us."

"I go, I go, swifter than arrow from the Tartar's bow." Puck spun around in circles, his skin shimmering as he shifted into a beautiful little sprite with gossamer wings and slipped into the fireplace. From somewhere up the chimney, I heard a high-pitched cough.

Are you sure that was a good idea? Quoth asked. *We could have kept him with us, been his alibi. The police know that people who stumble onto a crime scene often compromise it.*

"And what do you think Puck will do if Hayes takes him in for questioning?" I asked. "We might be able to convince Hiram Abernathy he hallucinated being a donkey, but I don't think that story will fly when the station CCTV captures Wilson transforming into a baboon. We need to keep this murder strictly in the human realm – the less Nevermore Bookshop insanity Hayes is exposed to, the faster he'll crack this case and find the real killer."

"Oh, so it's Hayes' job to solve this murder?" Heathcliff raised a bushy eyebrow. "Not a certain inquisitive bookstore half-owner turned vampire-slaying amateur sleuth?"

"I'm staying out of this." I folded my arms and glared at Heathcliff. "We have no reason to be involved. My murder-solving days are over."

"I could wipe down the book," Morrie said. "Get rid of the evidence Puck was here."

"No, then it will wipe off the killer's fingerprints, too." I wasn't going to help cover up a murder just to save Puck's bacon. The fairy had been trouble enough already. "Maybe fairy fingerprints don't show up in the human world—"

"Croak?"

"Quoth, what's up?" I cried out as the raven took off for the staircase. As he disappeared around the curve, I heard a series of quiet thuds, followed by a shout of surprise and more croaks.

Someone was up there.

The killer.

And he's got Quoth.

CHAPTER FOURTEEN

"Quoth!" I yelled, rushing to the staircase. Heathcliff got there first, but before he could charge our foe, a figure appeared on the landing, his fuzzy slippers making a slapping sound on the oak floorboards.

"Hello?" he called downstairs, his voice bleary. I recognized the voice of Rasmussen's apprentice, Lawrence Delacroix. Footsteps sounded on the stairs. "Jasper, is that you? You're up early. I think we have a bird in the fireplace. I'll call a fellow about it this morning—oh."

Lawrence stopped mid-step, directly beneath the single bulb in the stairwell. He wore a set of salmon-colored pajamas, the front misbuttoned, and a matching sleeping cap with a pompom dangling beside his ear. He peered around at us with confusion.

"Hello, there. What are you all doing in the shop? We don't open until 9AM. And where's Jasper?"

"He's right here, thou dissembling harlot." Heathcliff grabbed Lawrence by the collar and dragged him down the stairs, holding him over the body. "But don't expect him to be up to his old tricks anytime soon. He's gone to the great bookshop in the sky. Although I bet you knew that already, you leathern-jerkin, crystal-button, knot-pated, agate-ring, puke-stocking, caddis-garter, smooth-tongue, Spanish pouch—"

"Heathcliff," I warned.

"You must work on your diction, if you're to quote Shakespeare. I should know. I was Titus Andronicus in college… Jasper?" Lawrence's lips wobbled. His eyes filled with tears. "He's not dead, is he? He can't be dead."

"Now, now, Lawrence. You know you mustn't play pretend." Morrie stepped up to him, his voice dripping with menace. "I'm the *real* actor in the room, and I can see right through your charade. Why did you kill Rasmussen? He wasn't paying you enough? He stole your girlfriend? He refused to cut you in on whatever scheme he was involved in—"

"I didn't do this, I swear." Lawrence's voice wavered. Tears glistened on his cheeks. "I would never hurt him. He was a great man. He loved Shakespeare, just like I did, although he never had any acting experience like me. He was…he was the most important person in the world to me. If that bird could talk, he'd tell you that I'm innocent."

It's true, Quoth said as he fluttered down from upstairs and settled on my shoulder. *I found him upstairs, asleep in bed. And look how upset he is; it doesn't seem like he's the killer.*

Lawrence sniffed, his whole body racked with sobs. Quoth was right – this wasn't premeditated murder, it was a sudden decision, an act of rage and passion. The person who did this wouldn't be the kind of person who could put on a convincing show of grief. Lawerence's distress was real, I was certain of it.

Also, Oscar wasn't barking at him, which he would if he considered Lawrence a threat. And if Quoth, who had such a profound ability to see into the hearts of people, agreed, then…

"I don't think he's the murderer," I said. "Even though he was Titus Andronicus in college."

"Arf," Oscar agreed.

"Then if you didn't kill him, what are you doing here?" I demanded.

"I live here," he shot back. "Mr. Rasmussen is renting me his spare room upstairs until I can secure my own flat in the village. Or rather, he *was* renting me the room…what will I do without him?"

He swayed on his feet. I lunged for him, but I got tangled in Oscar's harness and didn't make it before Lawrence fainted in Heathcliff's arms.

Morrie reached around him and lifted the shop's phone receiver, dialing a number that was familiar to all of us by now.

"Inspector Hayes? Yes, it's James Moriarty. You might want to call in an extra order of doughnuts from Oliver and get over to Rasmussen Books. You've got another stiff."

*W*ord of Rasmussen's untimely demise spread through the village like, well, like village gossip usually spread. Less than ten minutes after we emerged into the deserted street, the whole place filled up with nosy villagers wanting to rubberneck the latest crime scene.

Such was our reputation for attracting murder in Argleton that a *second* crowd gathered outside the deserted Nevermore Bookshop, cupping their hands against the glass windows to peer inside. Apparently, they heard about a murder at a bookshop and jumped to the obvious conclusion.

I gazed up at the tops of the buildings, searching for a sign of the tiny sprite even though I knew I'd never be able to see him. *Please let Puck be far away by now. Please let him find a new home in an enchanted forest somewhere, so he can stop causing mischief in my life.*

"Mina, I'm relieved to see you." Mrs. Ellis wrapped her arms around me, her carpetbag slapping my shoulder. "I heard that a bookseller died, and I dropped everything and came running—"

"We're all fine. Just a little shaken up. We went to talk to Rasmussen about supplying him with books for the festival, and instead we found his body." I shuddered at the memory. "It was awful."

"Oh dear. And let me guess, the police assume you're the killers?"

"What makes you so sure he was murdered?" Heathcliff cut in, peering at her with suspicion.

"*Please*, this is Argleton," Mrs. Ellis tsked. "We live in a typical English murder village. No one dies of natural causes here. They're either impaled with garden trowels by disgruntled neighbors or poisoned by elderflower wine at the fete or exsanguinated by literary vampires come to life. What I want to know is, will I have to spring you from jail so we can chase down the killer and bring them to justice? I've been practicing opening locks with my crochet hooks…"

"I don't think we'll need your services at this time," I said, trying to hide a giggle. "We'll be staying well out of this investigation. It's time the Argleton police did their own work."

I've got more important things to do than solve this case, like helping my birdie find his wings again.

"Right you are, my girl. Still, it's all so terrible," Mrs. Ellis shook her head sadly. "I didn't like the man, of course. But he was a tremendous asset to the festival. Do you know what will happen to the First Folio now that he's gone?"

I shrugged. "It will be the property of his heir, I suspect. Although there was a bloodstain on the book, so the police might need to hold it as evidence."

Mrs. Ellis winced. "Oooh, Miles won't like that. Speaking of our valiant leader, here he is now."

"Mina. Mabel." Miles came running up to us, gasping for air. "I came as soon as I heard. This is an absolute disaster. The press are swarming all over the place and I see all our investors in the crowd here – the festival is doomed."

Odd. I wonder why Miles is puffing like he ran over from the theater. We saw him just across the green a few minutes ago. Surely he hadn't made it to the theater yet?

"I'm sure it's not as bad as all that," I said. "You've put together a wonderful program, and the New New Globe is such a good idea. Once people see the performances and experience theater the way Shakespeare intended—"

Miles shook his head. "That's if anyone even comes to the performances now. Everyone is saying the festival is cursed! All this work to put together something wonderful, all the support the village has given us and the hours of volunteer labor, and the only thing people will remember about our festival is that someone was murdered."

Miles loped off, looking glum.

Quoth's talons dug into my shoulder. I followed his gaze to the door of Rasmussen's shop. Lawrence Delacroix stood on the steps, staring in gape-mouthed shock as police officers and the SOCO team entered the building. Tears rolled silently down his gaunt cheeks and splashed on his misbuttoned pajamas. It was hard for me to understand, but he must've admired Mr. Rasmussen a great deal to be so affected by his murder—

"Arrrgh!"

An ear-piercing scream cut off my thought. People in the crowd leaped out of the way as someone shoved their way toward the bookshop.

"Daddy, *no.*" Shelley fell to her knees in the square, flailing her arms around and beating her fists against the town green. People shuffled away from her, confused by her outpouring of grief as only British people can be in the presence of unrepressed emotion.

Now, this does seem like an awful lot of tears for someone who earlier was telling us how much she was done with her father. And Shelley would probably have her own key to the shop and—

No, stop it. It's Hayes' turn to solve a murder in this village. You've already done enough.

As if on cue, Inspector Hayes stepped outside, lifting the crime scene tape and beckoning us over. "Mina Wilde, why am I not surprised you were first on the scene?"

"I swear this time we are completely innocent," I said. "We came to talk to Mr. Rasmussen about buying some of our Shakespeare stock for the festival and found him like this. We didn't touch a thing except picking up the book, which Morrie did with gloves."

I gave Hayes as much detail as I could about the lead-up to us discovering Rasmussen's body. I left out the bit about Puck being with us. Hopefully, when Hayes spoke to the other witnesses, they wouldn't remember him.

Hayes scratched his head. "A lot of people had business with Rasmussen this morning. Zenzile Monroe has confessed to being in the square this morning, but she claims the shop door was locked so she never went inside. She also made no secret of the fact that she despised the man," Hayes said. "We all heard her last night."

"Yes, but that was *Shakespeare*, it's supposed to be dramatic. And I saw both Shelley Rasmussen and Hiram Abernathy in the square, too." I left out the bit about Hiram's newfound love for hay.

"And we should be suspects, too," Morrie piped up. He sounded hopeful.

I glared at him. "What are you doing?"

"Well, if we're being honest, it *could* have been us." Morrie's eyes glinted. "We have motive – the guy stole Nevermore's spot as the festival bookseller. And we were the ones to find his body."

"Are you making a confession, Mr. Moriarty?" Hayes asked.

Was it my imagination, or was there a touch of hope in Hayes' voice?

Morrie grinned. "And ruin all the fun of you catching me? Never."

Inspector Hayes sighed. "I'd *like* to think that with all your experience of murder, you'd know better than to clobber the guy with a giant book in broad daylight, so no, you're not serious suspects. But we have to do this by the book," he cringed. "Sorry for the pun, but please don't leave the village without telling me, okay?"

"Got it."

Hayes turned back to the site. I touched my phone, which read out the time. 8:46AM. "We should get back and open the shop."

"Why?" Heathcliff pouted. "People are going to hang out here all day hoping for grisly details. No one will be in buying literature."

"They will if we redo all the window displays with true crime books. Now, come on." I shoved Heathcliff in the general direction of the shop.

The moment we entered Nevermore, Quoth transformed from his raven form. He sat on the edge of the table, nervously patting the stuffed armadillo as he dangled his bare feet. "Mina, I think we *should* solve this murder."

"We can't." I shook my head. "I promised Hayes we were staying out of this one."

Quoth glanced over his shoulder. "Yes, but...you know they're going to make a mess of this case. Hell, they might even say the poor man tripped and dropped the First Folio on his head multiple times."

I snorted, but Quoth wasn't joking.

"I just think that we could help bring the killer to justice."

I looked into his eyes and saw something swimming there.

Pain. For some reason, Rasmussen's death had become personal to Quoth.

"Why do you *really* want to do this?" I asked, taking his hand and squeezing it.

"Because...because I hurt people," he finished, staring at our fingers entwined. "If it weren't for me, Dracula might not have killed Miriam and Dana for their dirt. And Mrs. Ellis, Fiona, your mum, and you, my beautiful Mina – you all nearly died because of me."

"Quoth, none of that is your fault. You weren't in control of yourself. We all have terrible things in our past that we're not proud of, but we have to forgive ourselves. You are not your actions. You don't have to be ashamed of who you are."

"I do." He looked away. "I can't stop thinking that everyone I love would be better off if they'd never met me. That's why Jo's gone away. She can't bear to look at me, and I can't say I blame her."

"That's not true. Jo and Fiona have gone on a much-deserved holiday."

But even as I said it, Jo's words from our last conversation replayed in my mind. "It's not that I don't adore Quoth, but it's hard to be in the same room with him and know that he helped a bloodthirsty vampire come after my girl. Fiona and I just need to get away from Argleton and Nevermore Bookshop for a couple of weeks."

"It is true. I can read it on your face." Quoth's shoulders sagged. "And I understand completely. I can't bear to look at myself, either. But if I can do something good, if I can save the festival from this murderer, then maybe I'll feel like I have some redemption."

"We could plant trees?" I said. "Or volunteer at the animal shelter..."

But Quoth already did those things. *And* he cooked meals for Earl Larson and the local homeless population. *And* he'd been teaching an art class for kids on the housing estate where I grew up. Good deeds weren't helping him forgive himself, so why did he think solving a murder would?

Quoth squeezed my hand. "The village *needed* this festival, Mina. They needed a big, sparkly, fun event to show them that the world wasn't just a terrifying place. Look at you, look at the way you threw yourself into the costumes and the bookshop displays the moment Mrs. Ellis came knocking. You needed this festival, too. And saving it is what I need to do to heal."

I glanced out the window, where two shapes that could only be Hayes and Wilson were moving back across the green. Hayes' words echoed in my head.

I sighed. "Okay, we're doing this. Where should we begin?"

CHAPTER FIFTEEN

*W*hile Quoth flew over to Rasmussen Books to eavesdrop on the police investigation, I took a tiny silver key from Morrie's sex toy drawer and headed across the street to let myself into Mrs. Ellis' old flat.

Morrie purchased the building from Grey Lachlan after the developer had been cured of Dracula's hold on him, but he still hadn't decided what to do with it. In the meantime, I commandeered the breakfast nook as a writing studio and sewing room. When the shop was quiet enough that Heathcliff could be trusted in the presence of customers, I came over here to work on my book.

I hadn't done as much writing lately because I'd been working on the costumes, but with Rasmussen's murder fresh in my mind, I thought it might be the perfect time to edit the scene where I first discovered Ashley's body.

Over the last year, I'd been writing the story of how Heathcliff, Morrie, Quoth and I first met and fell in love, and the very first murder we solved together – that of my ex-best friend, Ashley Greer. At first, it was just a new hobby to take my mind off not being able to do fashion any longer, but more and more I found myself daydreaming about holding one of my own books in my hands and seeing it on the shelves at the bookshop alongside my other favorite authors.

I didn't like to write while the guys were around, because I was terrified they'd want to read it and it would be terrible and they'd tell me so (Morrie), or worse, trip over themselves trying to spare my feelings (Heathcliff and Quoth). It was amazing what a little peace and quiet did for my creativity. In the last two months since I'd been writing in the empty building, I'd blitzed through the first draft, and I was now editing and tweaking – trying to get every scene perfect and every emotion exactly as I remembered it.

I'd even sent off the first three chapters to the prestigious Meddleworth House Trust to consider me for their annual writers' retreat. Writers from all over the country applied to spend a week in the famous country estate being tutored by award-winning British authors. I didn't believe I had a chance in hell, but you never knew until you applied.

I was bent over my beaten-up old laptop (covered in band stickers, because of course), typing away, when a black shape fluttered down from the rafters and landed beside me, dunking his beak into my now-cold mug of tea. A moment later, Quoth's warm leg pressed against mine as he sank, naked, into the chair beside me. Reluctantly, I set aside my manuscript and turned my attention to him.

"Did you hear anything useful?" I asked.

"I heard *everything*." He sounded quite pleased with himself.

"You're telling me you sat up in the corner of Rasmussen's shop this whole time and no one even thought to question it?"

So much for our observant police force.

"I even stole the marshmallow from Wilson's hot chocolate." Quoth shrugged. "Maybe Inspector Hayes assumes all bookshops have a resident raven, so he didn't think it odd. I don't know. Anyway, do you want to know what I heard?"

I pulled over the whiteboard we used as a murder board, handing him the pen. "Please."

"First of all, Jo's temporary replacement is a real hard-ass. But he had an assistant with him who was absolutely lovely. She even snuck me a handful of nuts from her lunch when no one was looking. Remember the name George Fisher, because she's moving up in the world."

"Noted."

"Second, time of death was approximately ten or twenty minutes before we entered the shop. The rear entrance was locked from the inside and the downstairs windows painted shut, so it's definitely possible we passed the murderer when we walked across the square."

"Phew," I said. "That's a little terrifying. Just think, if Puck hadn't turned Hiram into an ass, we might've walked in on the murderer in the middle of their desperate act."

"Exactly. This brings me to points three and four. You were right about the murderer being someone he knew. They found no evidence of a break-in, and Wilson made a big point about would-be thieves not leaving a two-million quid book behind, not to mention the other valuable items on display that haven't been touched."

Quoth wrote this down on the whiteboard.

"What about point four?" I asked.

"I was getting to that. There's a question mark around the unlocked front door. Zen says that when she tried the door, it was locked. Lawrence swore he checked everything was locked before he went to sleep, and he claimed Rasmussen wouldn't normally leave the door unlocked outside of opening hours. That and the tea and biscuits suggest he was expecting a guest and opened the door for them. But if that's true, how could someone enter the building between Zen and us without us seeing them?"

"Unless Zen is lying about the lock," I said as Quoth scribbled down more notes. "Carry on."

"The First Folio is definitely the murder weapon," Quoth said. "He was struck with it at least three times – twice on the head, as we saw, and once on the shoulder – probably a swing that missed."

"So, he was definitely *attacked.*"

"Exactly. And sixthly…"

RAP RAP RAP.

"Who's that rapping at our chamber door?" Quoth asked as he stood to peer out the window.

RAP RAP RAP.

"That's not coming from our front door." I picked up Oscar's harness and joined Quoth at the window. The sound was coming from across the street. Oscar leaped onto the windowsill, pawing at the glass and whimpering as Hayes and Wilson hammered on the locked bookshop door.

Good luck with that, officers. If he was in one of his moods, Heathcliff wouldn't even open that door for a traveling whisky salesman.

Quoth ducked behind the couch, covering his bits with a pile of books just as Hayes spotted us in the window and came over. He jabbed his thumb at the bookshop. "Mina! It's Hayes. You need to make him open this door."

"What's going on?" I glanced down at Quoth.

He shrugged. "That's the sixth thing I wanted to tell you. They're here to take Puck in for questioning. They think he's the murderer."

CHAPTER SIXTEEN

"*U*nhand me, villains," Puck yelled as the police escorted him out of the bookshop. A crowd gathered on the street, because this was Argleton and they had nowhere else to be, and they whispered amongst themselves as Wilson shoved Puck into her squad car.

"He's always been a strange one," said Deirdre from the post office. "Why, just last week I caught him at the pub. He'd swiped Harriet Wistledown's stool and knelt on the floor so she sat on his back! And then he toppled over, and down fell she! Her skirts went up over her head and you could see her petticoat. He thought it hilarious, but poor Harriet was beet red for days."

"Mind you, they always attract the oddest people to that bookshop," said her friend. "Remember the social media star who only wore bedsheets and spouted New Age nonsense in the streets?"

If you consider Classical Greece the New Age, I wanted to shout, wishing I had Heathcliff's insult book on hand.

Quoth – who was stressed enough that he'd transformed back into his raven form – dug his talons into my shoulder and nodded his head in agitation.

"I bet that scary Heathcliff put him up to it," sniffed Tom the butcher. "Mark my words, he's the mastermind behind this. A new bookshop comes to town and suddenly the owner is *conveniently* knocked off, just in time for Nevermore to swoop in and save the day? I don't believe in coincidences, not after all the murders that have been connected to that place. And have you seen his cold, dead eyes? Cross Heathcliff Earnshaw and you're a dead man."

Oh, no you don't. No one is going to blame my Heathcliff for this murder.

Mina, wait— Quoth flapped his wings, trying to distract me, but I ducked under him and urged Oscar toward the door.

"Mina, wait—"

I burst outside, waving my arms around to draw their attention from the departing police cars. "You've got it all wrong. This isn't Heathcliff's fault, and it's not Puck's, either. I know he's a bit of a trickster, but he's not malicious. The police have no evidence that he's the murderer. You can't condemn a man before he's even had a fair trial—"

"He turned me into a donkey," Hiram Abernathy yelled. "If that ain't malicious, then I—"

Beside him, Dolores thumped him on the back of the head. "You shut your pie hole, Hiram Abernathy, and stop blaming another man because you were hiding in the stables from your breakfast smoothie."

"Exactly. Thank you, Dolores," I said. "Obviously, no one has the power to turn someone into a donkey. And Puck *will* have his name cleared of this murder, you'll see. Now, unless you want to buy some Shakespeare books, I suggest you get out of here because the vein over Heathcliff's eye is popping and—"

I didn't have to say another word. The crowd scattered, although I could hear them muttering and mumbling as they wandered away.

This village is too bloody suggestible.

Oscar and I scrambled up the steps to the shop. Quoth fluttered in over our heads. I slammed the door shut behind us and turned the sign to CLOSED. "Heathcliff, Morrie, get your asses in here. We have a big problem."

Heathcliff thundered down the stairs, his face red with rage. "You were magnificent out there," he hissed in my ear as he took my arm and led me into the main room.

"Croooak." Quoth dive-bombed behind Heathcliff's desk, and a moment later I heard him in his human form hunting for the stash of clothing he kept there.

Morrie pranced in front of the window, wearing his Macbeth costume and attempting to swordfight against an invisible enemy. When he saw us, he dropped the weapon and rubbed his hands together with glee. "You've got that expression on your face, gorgeous. Let me guess – we're going to solve a murder."

"Oh, no, we're not," Heathcliff snapped. "Mina promised that we're hanging up our crime-solving boots. This shop is a murder-free zone."

"We might not have a choice," I said, with a glance at Quoth, who leaned against the desk and hid behind a curtain of silken hair. "Hayes just arrested Puck."

Morrie slapped his forehead. "I knew we should have wiped his prints from the book."

"But how would they get Puck's prints to compare to the book?" Heathcliff said. "He might be an annoying rapscallion, but he hasn't caused enough trouble to have a rap sheet."

"You remember a month ago, when Richard gave Puck that bartending job at the pub, and he swapped the beer for spinach juice?" Quoth asked.

"Oh, yes, that was hilarious," Morrie said.

"It was not," Heathcliff snapped. "I was thirsty."

"It turns out, Wilson didn't think it was so funny, either. I overheard her telling Hayes that she thought Puck was bad news so she dusted his pint glass for prints and added them to the system."

"Is she allowed to do that? Just take any old person's prints without their consent?"

"Who knows? That's for lawyers to argue about in court. The point is that they've arrested Puck, which means they won't be looking for the real killer. What are we going to do?" I slumped into Heathcliff's chair and dropped my head into my hands.

There was a weird sound, like glitter falling from the sky, and then Heathcliff said, "I don't think we need to worry about Puck."

"Of course we do. He may be annoying, but he's our responsibility and—"

"Turn around, gorgeous."

I whirled around.

I blinked twice as my eyes adjusted to the lighting. Sitting on top of the poetry shelf, his hands covered in fingerprinting ink, was Puck.

"Annoying, am I?" he grinned impishly. "Would an annoying Puck do *this*?"

From behind his back, he produced a bunch of wildflowers, which he held out to me.

"AAAH-CHOO."

Heathcliff slapped his hands over his mouth. The entire bookstore trembled. Oscar whimpered and hid behind my leg.

Puck's lip wobbled.

Heathcliff grabbed the flowers and hurled them out the window.

"I mistook. But would an annoying Puck do this—"

Heathcliff closed his fist over Puck's hand before he could cause any more disasters.

"We're not blaming you for this," I said to Puck. "But here's the thing. You can't be seen in Argleton. The police don't take too kindly to anyone disappearing from their custody. They're going to come screaming down the street any minute to search for you, and if you're here when they do, you'll get us all into trouble. And unlike you, we can't magic ourselves out of a prison cell."

Puck looked like he was about to argue, but one look from Heathcliff and his shoulders sagged. "So far blameless proves my enterprise. But what should I do?"

A knock sounded at the door. "Mina, Heathcliff. Open up immediately." It was Wilson, and she sounded *pissed*.

Heathcliff grabbed Puck's wrists and waved them in the air. "Cast your fairy dust and disappear. I don't know why we tried to help you. You're unfit for any place but hell."

Puck hung his head. "As you wish," he murmured, his shoulders slumping as though Heathcliff's words had truly stung him. "Up and down, up and down, I will lead them up and down. I am feared in field and town. Goblin, lead them—"

"Just go," Heathcliff growled. And with a *POP* and a sparkle, Puck disappeared just as the police jimmied our ancient lock and stormed into the shop.

"Mina, there you are." Hayes leaned over the desk, breathing hard. He sounded like he'd run all the way here from the station. Behind him, Wilson folded her arms. "We need to talk to you about this Puck fellow. He's done a runner from our custody."

"That's terrible news," Morrie said.

"It is, it is." Hayes scratched his head. "I've never seen anything like it. It was as if he just vanished by magic. The lock wasn't even tampered with. And it reminds me of that night *you* disappeared from custody, Mina. I know this Puck is a friend of yours. He put this bookshop down as his place of residence, so I'm hoping you can help me here."

"Just tell us where he's hiding," Wilson said, "and we'll go easy on you."

She didn't sound like she'd do anything of the sort.

Morrie shrugged. "I'm afraid we're as baffled as you are. Mina's escape was purely opportunistic – and she caught the real killer, so no harm done. Puck isn't staying here. He just says that because he wants to get us in trouble. As for disappearing, he has form. He's a magician."

Good one, Morrie.

"A magician?" Hayes sounded skeptical.

"Sure," I nodded vigorously. "He disappears for a living. It's part of his routine. I mean, only a magician would voluntarily call themselves Puck."

"Well, how did he do it? Because I've got CCTV footage of him vanishing into thin air and escaping from a locked cell, and I'm baffled as to how that's possible."

"Alas, a magician never reveals his tricks, not even to his friends. Might I suggest you look carefully at the League of Cunning Conjurers – the premier London magic society."

"You think he's gone to London?"

"I think," Morrie said, "that if I were on the run from the law, I'd want to hang out with a bunch of fellows who make it their business to pull live rabbits from dark nether regions where no rabbit should ever be."

Hayes waved a finger in Morrie's face. "Very well. If I hear even so much as a *whisper* that you or Mina or Mr. Earnshaw had anything to do with this, you'll all be in jail, got it?"

"We promise we'll be good," Morrie said sweetly.

Hayes and Wilson left. But before Heathcliff could storm after them and shut the door, a new customer ran in. He slammed into the desk, gasping for air.

"Good, you're open again. I want to know if you have any books by…" he checks his phone for a moment. "Stella Mey."

"I'm sorry, we've sold out of her."

"Um…sure. Well, can you call me if you get any in?" He handed me a card. "I mean, like the *very minute* someone drops one off, I'd like a call. I'll pay extra for the service."

"Are you a big Mey fan?" He certainly didn't seem like the type to go wild for young adult vampire novels, but I'd worked in a bookshop long enough to know readers would always surprise you.

"I will be if I can get my hands on her books." The guy scribbled his number down and left.

"That's the fourth person who's asked for books by Stella Mey this week," Heathcliff said. "They've all been desperate, and yet none of them seem to have any idea who she is."

I turned to Heathcliff. "It's strange, but this almost smacks of—"

"Mina, darling!"

Mum's voice echoed through the shop. Heathcliff gave a terrified yelp and scuttled away into his office, slamming the door behind him. Mum swept in, wearing her sequined witch dress with a full-length fur coat and a pair of winged sunglasses. I choked back a laugh as I leaned in to hug her. I ran my fingers through the fur and felt bare patches, and the coat had a musty smell that suggested she'd just purchased it from the Argleton village charity shop.

"How now, you secret black and midnight hag?" Morrie leaned in to kiss my mother's cheeks. "Are you all ready for opening night?"

"Of course." She whipped off her sunglasses and twirled in her ridiculous outfit. "I've been wearing my costume everywhere, Mina, just in case the paparazzi snap me. I could get your name in the paper, then you'd be rich and famous."

"Thanks, Mum, that's really thoughtful of you," I said. With Mum, it was best to let a few of her less-insane ideas slide. "How's the vampire-hunting kit business going?"

"Oh, that's ancient history." Mum waved her hand. "After October I couldn't sell a vampire-hunting kit to save my life. Andy and I have a new business now, and the best thing about it is that it benefits *you*."

I was a hundred percent certain that it didn't. "Um, Mum, maybe you should—"

"Sold out of Stella Mey's books, I see." Mum winked at me as she pointed to an empty space on the shelf.

Yup, called it. "Mum, what did you do?"

She leaned in close, her hand cupped over her mouth in a conspiratorial whisper. "I'm the Book Whisperer."

"The what?"

"The Book Whisperer. Surely you've heard of me?" Mum looked affronted. "I'm all over TikTok."

"Oh Mina," Morrie held up his phone. "You have got to see this app I found."

I grabbed the phone off him and tapped at the screen. Mum's face grinned back at me in a short video. She was dressed the way she was now, sparkly dress, winged sunglasses, and threadbare fur coat, waving her hands over a crystal ball. "The Book Whisperer tells you that Stella Mey will die a terrible, tragic death in five years, three months, and eighteen days, making her books an excellent investment. But not as good as Steffanie Holmes, the steamy romance author who has been eating one too many chocolate biscuits and is about to discover that one of them is poisoned—"

"Mum, what *is* this?"

"I heard how stressed you were about that bloke across the green opening his competing bookshop, so I thought I'd drum up a little extra business for you," Mum explained. "He gave me the idea, actually. Him and his fancy collectible books. I had no idea how much money you could make from dusty old books!"

"Yes, Mum, but that's not what you're doing."

"Of course not. Who wants to spend hours hunting down dusty old books," Mum scoffed. "My business is much better. It's really very simple. I predict which famous author will die next, and then people buy up all their books in anticipation of their imminent demise, in the hopes that those books will be worth more once they're deceased."

Mum threw her arms wide, as if she were waiting for our

applause.

"Mum, you can't do this. What if these authors don't die? Or what if they *do* die? You'd be profiting off their demise. That's…immoral."

"Why not?" Mum grinned. "That new bookshop across the square profits from the work of long-dead writers and no one bats an eyelid. What's the difference?"

"The difference is…is…that the new shop owner is *dead*. Someone *murdered* him. You're playing in a dangerous field, so perhaps you should stop now before—"

"Mina, please, if I let every little murder in this village sway me from my path, I wouldn't be the successful entrepreneur I am today." Mum frowned at her phone. "Such a pity he chose to pop his clogs today. I never thought to extend my predictions to the people who sell books. I wonder how long your Heathcliff will be around, what with all the booze he swills…"

"If *any* of our names show up in this app of yours, Mum, I swear that I'll…I'll…" I couldn't think of a punishment. "I'll sic Heathcliff on you."

"Hey, don't bring me into this," Heathcliff yelled from his office.

Mum patted my arm. "Honestly, Mina, you worry too much. I must be off, darling. You'll thank me when you're rolling in cash. I see you've got lots of Damon Slaughter thrillers over there – I shall do my next video on him. Morrie, I shall see you tonight for our stage debut."

Before I could say another word, she breezed past me, leaving a cloud of perfume and a vague sense of unease behind her.

Between Quoth's crusade to solve the murder and forgive himself, Morrie's campaign to curse the production, and my mother's attempts to help with our precarious financial situation, my life had suddenly become a Shakespearean play.

I just hoped it wasn't going to be a tragedy, where everyone died at the end.

CHAPTER SEVENTEEN

*W*e knew Hayes and Wilson would be spending the day interviewing all the people we'd seen in the square and going on their wild goose chase to find Puck. So Quoth and I decided to start with another avenue of inquiry. We had three names on our suspect list – three people who we saw in the square that morning and who were angry with Mr. Rasmussen for various reasons. We didn't have enough to narrow down our suspects or establish a clear motive, but we knew *exactly* where to go to get the gossip on their lives.

Our first stop was Oliver's bakery, where we stocked up on his famous jam doughnuts. "Did you see anything in the square this morning?" I asked Oliver as he packed our treats into a box and wrapped up a sausage roll for Oscar.

"You mean aside from the donkey knocking over my sign?" Oliver asked.

"Technically, he wasn't a donkey, but an ass," Quoth said with a shy smile in his voice.

"Speaking of asses, that American chap came in, demanding I make him up a box of treats even though I told him we didn't open for another twenty minutes," Oliver said. "He kept looking over his shoulder while I filled his box, barking at me to go faster."

"What did he order? Let me guess… a dozen jam doughnuts?" I asked. "Mince pie and chips?"

"He had a big red stain on his collar," Quoth explained. "We assumed it was from something he ate here."

Oliver shook his head. "Nothing to do with my food. He didn't order anything with tomato sauce or jam in it. Mainly fairy cakes and cheese scones. He got that stain somewhere else."

Like, say, from Rasmussen's blood splashing on his collar as he clobbered him with the First Folio?

Oliver handed over our box. It smelled amazing, but I managed to resist opening it and gobbling half the contents before we reached our destination. Oscar and I had to jog to keep up with Quoth, who raced across the cricket pitch toward the New New Globe. "Mrs. Ellis," I called out as I swung open the stage door. "We come bearing treats."

As we entered the backstage area, Mrs. Ellis and her friends sprung apart, their faces painted with guilt. "Mina, Allan, what a surprise. We didn't expect to see you until later today, what with all the excitement in the village."

"What are you all doing here?" Quoth asked shyly, even though we knew exactly why they were there. "We don't need actors until the evening call time."

"Oh, well, um," Cynthia Lachlan babbled. "You see, we were—"

"You were just gossiping about Mr. Rasmussen's murder, was what you were doing," I said as I swung a chair around and plonked down the bakery box. "And we want to know everything."

CHAPTER EIGHTEEN

"*Y*ou know," Mrs. Ellis said as she bit into her third jam doughnut. "You two make much better investigators than that dolt Inspector Hayes. He doesn't think our information is very useful."

"We told him that your friend Puck was a perfectly harmless young man," added Sylvia Blume, brushing crumbs off her velvet dress. "To think our taxpayer dollars are being wasted on this farce when the real killer is still out there. Imagine believing that delightful young man could turn someone into a donkey? It's absurd—"

Beside me, Quoth made a choking noise. His gaze flicked to a spot behind Mrs. Ellis' head. Moments later, a pair of invisible hands twisted Mrs. Ellis' blue-rinsed hair up into twin devil horns.

Puck was in the house.

"We know that between Inspector Hayes' ears is a wad of cotton," said Mrs. Ellis. "Why, he didn't even want to hear my theory that the murderer is a crazed Shakespeare fan determined to reenact the Bard's most celebrated slayings. Hasn't anyone taught that young man he should listen to his elders?"

I laughed at the idea of Hayes, with his greying hair and tired eyes, being considered young.

Quoth poured Sylvia another glass of tea. "You always have such deep insights," he said in his soft, kind voice. "I think if anyone could see into the heart of our killer, it would be you."

"Why, thank you for noticing, young man," Sylvia touched the crystal around her neck. "I do possess the gift of second sight, although there are many who doubt the validity of my visions."

With good reason, I thought but didn't say. *Sylvia's visions are the result of staring into an empty wine bottle, rather than any psychic gifts.*

Sylvia rubbed her temples and hummed under her breath. Quoth sat forward, utterly enraptured with her performance. My birdie had a way of making people feel special so they would relax and open up around him. Sylvia watched Quoth's expression with relish as she slapped the table with her palm and announced, "The spirits have spoken to me, and they tell me that the police should be looking more carefully at Zenzile Monroe."

"Oh, I don't know, Sylvia," said Hazel Barrowly as she licked jam and cream off her fingers. "Zen may have hated the man, but I can't imagine her defacing that precious book by splattering it with his blood."

"I can, if she was desperate enough." Mrs. Ellis rubbed her hands together with glee. "Did you know the council is threatening to shut down the Shakespeare Museum?"

I leaned forward. *This is it. This is what we came for. No one knows the sordid underbelly of the village like Mrs. Ellis and her old biddies.* "Is that so?"

"I heard all about it at last month's community meeting. They've kept it open this long because of its cultural value, but the new mayor is cutting costs and he doesn't want a money pit on the books. That museum is Zen's life. She's understandably devastated. And if she could get Rasmussen to donate his First Folio, then the place would stay open."

"But wouldn't that be a reason to keep the guy alive, not to brutally clobber him to death?"

"Not necessarily." Sylvia reached for another doughnut. "The spirits are unclear on her motives, but Zen might have become enraged when he refused to donate the book, and hit him in desperation, not realizing her blow would strike him dead."

"Or perhaps it was a calculated attack?" Mrs. Ellis suggested. "Zen knew Shelley Rasmussen supported donating the First Folio. If she knocked off Jasper, then Shelley would inherit the business and give Zen the book."

Desperation or premeditation? I remembered when we ran into Zen in the square, and how flustered she appeared. It could have been shock at what she'd done, or an attempt to hide her crime with a little hammy acting. She said she'd been to see Rasmussen, but the door was locked. Yet minutes later, we found the door open. She could have been lying to us.

"But she's not the only one in financial turmoil," added Cynthia, leaning close to stage-whisper conspiratorially. "Grey tells me that Miles Stapleton mortgaged his house to pay for the construction of the New New Globe. He didn't even tell his wife he was doing it. If the festival bombs, he'll lose everything."

I couldn't believe Miles would do something so foolish. But did bad financial decisions make him a killer?

"If that's true, why would Miles kill Rasmussen?" Mrs. Ellis sipped her tea with the relish of Miss Marple looking over a particularly gruesome slaying. "This murder has brought negative press and financial instability to the festival, and that couldn't be worse for Miles. No, that doesn't make sense. But I don't think Zen committed this crime, either. If for no other reason than she'd never dare treat a First Folio with such disrespect. I think we should be looking at Mr. Hiram Abernathy and his wife Dolores."

"I met her this morning," I said. "She seemed lovely."

"Oh, she is. But she likes things to be a certain way, and she has Hiram shaking in his boots at the mere thought of displeasing her. Rumor has it that if he doesn't secure this book for her by her birthday today, she'll have his guts for garters. Perhaps the man got desperate, and when Mr. Rasmussen wouldn't sell, he became violent."

"He *is* a Texan," Cynthia mused. "They're famous for going off half-cocked."

The ladies collapsed into giggles.

"But again, hitting Rasmussen over the head doesn't seem like his style, either," Mrs. Ellis mused. "I'd half expect a cowboy-style shootout – pistols across the green at dawn."

"Again, he's a Texan. People in Texas make their tea with *ice* and *lemon slices.*" Cynthia wrinkled her nose as she cradled her teacup like it was a precious jewel. "You never know what people who are so cruel to tea would do."

"And what about Shelley Rasmussen?" Quoth said as he offered around the doughnuts. "She was seen on the green around the time of the murder, talking about how much she loved her father."

"Oh, yes, Shelley. Now she's a strange lass," said Hazel. "She's gone around with my Fergus, did you know? He said she's lovely enough, but there were too many things about her life he couldn't explain."

"Like what?" Quoth asked.

"You know, she lives on the estate and most of the time she doesn't have two pennies to rub together, but sometimes she'll show up with wads of cash. She even took my Fergus for a holiday to Ibiza last summer. She told him that her father was a rich bloke in London and he'd randomly get attacked by the guilts for neglecting her and send her money. Doesn't that seem a strange sort of father/daughter relationship to you?"

Actually, no. I wanted to say. *It's kind of normal for absentee parents to attempt to make up for being gone by throwing money at their offspring. Some of them even throw bookshops.*

"I wish my pa would randomly send me great wads of money," Sylvia let out a dramatic sigh. "All I get from him is exorbitant bills from the retirement home and occasional phone calls asking if I've seen where he put his dentures."

"My Fergus thought Shelley might be a drug dealer," Hazel said. "All that money in cash, and you know what sort of things they get up to on the estate. No offense meant, of course, Mina—"

I gritted my teeth but decided to let Hazel's comment about my home pass. As the ladies launched into a heated debate about the depths of debauchery to which Shelley Rasmussen may have sank, my stomach tightened in fear.

Quoth had all the village gossips eating out of the palm of his hand, but we were no closer to figuring out who murdered Jasper Rasmussen or why.

CHAPTER NINETEEN

*S*oon, the backstage area filled up with actors dressing and preparing for opening night, and for a couple of hours, I didn't have time to think about Mr. Rasmussen's murder because I was busy reattaching trim and tacking hems. Quoth, dressed head-to-toe in black and looking every bit like the lead singer of some hot, depressing goth band, flittered around the stage, getting the props and sets in place to be moved between scenes.

"The London press has booked out one of the Lord's Rooms," Quoth said as he shuffled past with Lady Macbeth's dagger for the prop table. He sounded nervous. I didn't blame him. I knew that the journalists were shaping their stories of the festival through the lens of Rasmussen's murder. We had to show them that in the village of Argleton, the show must go on.

"Fear not," Morrie cried as he strode into the room, kilt flapping and sword swinging. "It is I, Macbeth, here to save the show."

"Don't say that name!" cried Handy Andy, who was playing Macduff. He turned frantically in a circle.

"Oh, that's right." Morrie slapped his forehead. "I forgot I wasn't supposed to say Macbeth."

"Argh!" Cast members leaped from the makeup chairs and started doing wild dances around the room, chanting lines from the play that were supposed to undo the curse.

Morrie grinned wickedly as he sank into his designated makeup chair, and Sylvia set about transforming him into the Scottish king.

Heathcliff arrived a moment later, clad in black and smelling of peat and sweat and that delicious, unnameable Heathcliffness that made my knees weak. He'd been helping Quoth move some of the heavier sets into place, and he came over to kiss my cheek and peer at Morrie's kilt with a mixture of revulsion and desire.

"Are you ready to find a spot in the audience?" he asked as he squeezed my arm. "We can leave the scoundrel king to contemplate his various nefarious deeds."

"Fair is foul, and foul is fair." Morrie propped a leg up on the makeup table, giving Heathcliff a direct line of sight under his kilt. Judging by the way Heathcliff's body stiffened, Morrie was wearing his costume in the traditional Scottish way.

"Hold still," Sylvia tugged on Morrie's hair. "We're almost done."

"Curtain in five minutes," Miles called out as he stalked through the room, his voice trembling with nerves. "Places, everyone."

"What's that?" Heathcliff pointed to something stuck on the mirror.

"Oh, it's a note. It must be from one of my many admirers." Morrie grabbed it and unfolded the paper. He read the message aloud. "It says, 'I know you're investigating Rasmussen's murder. Meet me outside the stage door after the show. I have something important to tell you.' It's not signed."

"Do you recognize the writing?" I asked. "What about the stationery?"

"I don't care if it's from the bloody queen herself," Heathcliff growled. "We're not going to meet some anonymous note-leaver in a back alley. That's asking for exsanguination."

"But the note isn't threatening," I point out. "It just says that they have information, and maybe they're too afraid to talk to us in person. They must be someone in the cast or crew, because they placed the note on Morrie's mirror. Does that mean the killer is on the cast, too—"

"I will give all my fame for a pot of ale." Heathcliff tugged me toward the door. "It is of vital importance that we get to the bar before it closes."

"We'll deal with this after the show, gorgeous." Morrie adjusted his kilt and bent down to kiss me. "The stage is set, the lights are dimmed, and the crowd clamors for Macbeth!"

Everyone in the room groaned.

*M*orrie's wicked smile lit my heart as he disappeared into the wings. My job now done, Heathcliff, Oscar, and I snuck out the stage door and joined the people in the groundlings. Heathcliff went to get us drinks, and I leaned against the edge of the stage as the orange light illuminated the cauldron and the weird sisters' hag makeup and hooked prosthetic noses.

"When shall we three meet again," intoned my mother. "In thunder, lightning, or in rain?"

They plotted their meeting with our doomed king, and then the scene changed to a military camp, where King Duncan of Scotland received the news that his captains Macbeth and Banquo fought with great bravery, and Macbeth slew the traitor Macdonwald. In the next scene, the witches returned for another spell when Morrie strode on stage beside Oliver, who played Banquo. My criminal mastermind cut a magnificent Macbeth, resplendent in his sword and kilt as he drew his lovely wife into his web. Beside me, Heathcliff gritted his teeth, crushing his plastic cup in his big hand. My own mouth went dry, something about the confidence Morrie exuded as he strode around the stage, plotting his bloody path to the throne.

He was right – he was born to play Macbeth.

And Zen was pretty good, too. You could tell she loved the role and poured everything she had into being an authentically terrifying Lady Macbeth. And my mum and Cynthia and Mrs. Ellis as the witches had the audience in stitches with their antics.

I couldn't see Quoth when the lights were out, but I'd recognize his light footsteps anywhere as he helped the stage crew wheel on the sets and arrange props between scenes. The lights went up again, revealing the scene of Lady Macbeth's bedchamber, but she was nowhere to be seen.

Heathcliff pointed, and I gasped as I saw Zen, wearing a billowing white shift dotted with blood, wandering through the upper galleries and balcony, back and forth, rubbing frantically at her hands. The Doctor and Gentlewoman appeared on stage, and they talked about her descent into madness.

"Out, damned spot," Zen cried. "Out, I say…"

As she rubbed at her hands, her actions growing increasingly unhinged, she climbed over the edge of the gallery to stand on a narrow ledge directly above the groundlings. Her nightgown whipped around her legs as she lurched and wobbled three stories above our heads.

The crowd gasped. My chest tightened, but I told myself Zen was perfectly safe. I couldn't see the rigging beneath her dress, but I knew she'd been strapped into the system Morrie designed with mathematical precision to bring her safely down to earth.

In the play, Lady Macbeth's suicide happened offstage, but Mrs. Ellis decided that sex and violence sell tickets, so she wanted as much blood and gore on stage as possible. Zen's hair tangled about her face as she cried her lines. "Here's the smell of the blood still. All the perfumes of Arabia will not sweeten this little hand. Oh, oh, oh."

The lighting grew grim, tinged with red. She wrung her hands as the music crested, and she stepped over the edge.

Her words turned into a scream.

Something about that screen chilled my blood.

Her shriek cut off abruptly with a sickening *CRUNCH*.

The band fell silent.

The crowd stilled.

"I don't think that's stage blood," Heathcliff said.

I couldn't see, but I had to *know*. No one moved. No one else spoke.

We have to help her.

"Zen. Can you hear us?" I directed Oscar forward. Heathcliff looped his arm in mine and shoved his way through the stunned crowd. Behind us, I heard the familiar long stride of Morrie rushing across the stage to meet us.

Heathcliff dropped to his knees and pulled me down beside him. Zen was a dark lump on the ground, her legs bent at impossible angles. The air stank with the acrid tang of fresh blood. Heathcliff cradled her head in his lap. "You're going to be okay," he said gruffly.

I could tell from the bright tone in his voice that Zen was very, very far from okay.

"Mina…" she choked out, reaching out a bloodstained hand to me. "My note. You must—"

But she didn't get to finish her sentence.

Zen's head loped to the side. Heathcliff tapped her cheek, but she didn't respond.

She was gone.

CHAPTER TWENTY

"*S*he's dead," Heathcliff announced.

"Who knew the woman to have so much blood in her," Puck intoned, appearing beside us in a shower of sparkles.

"Do shut up," Heathcliff muttered. "And get out of here. The police are on their way."

"Now the hungry lion roars, and the wolf behowls the moon—"

"Go *away,* Puck." For once, Morrie wasn't in a joking mood. He stared down at the crumpled body, his shoulders hunched, his long fingers tugging at his sleeves. I knew he felt responsible – he designed the rigging, and it had failed at the worst possible moment.

Quoth pulled me close, wrapping his arms around me. I buried my face in his shoulder, letting his dark hair fall over my life like a curtain, hiding me from the horror.

We were on our own. As soon as the accident happened, Heathcliff and Morrie sprang into action. Because of the design of the New New Globe, there was no stage curtain we could pull down to hide Zen's body from view, so the next best thing was to get everyone outside. Heathcliff used his ineffable wit and charm (aka, his impressive bulk and threats of violence) to herd the terrified audience into the beer garden to wait for the police. Mrs. Ellis and her eagle-eyed volunteers were making sure no one left before they'd been questioned.

Which meant that no one was around to stop us sneaking a look at the scene. We shouldn't touch the body before the police arrived (at least, not any more than we already had, since her head was in Heathcliff's lap when she died), but Quoth couldn't be dissuaded. He bent over Zen, leaning in close to search for clues. Then he and Morrie inspected the rigging.

"At least I know there was no fault in my design," Morrie said. "See these carabiners? The ones I used are made of steel and designed to hold someone five times Zen's weight. But they've been replaced with cheap, flimsy ones. Look, when the rigging took Zen's weight, it snapped them clean in half."

"I checked them," Quoth said, his voice choked with tears. "I checked every element of the rigging this afternoon exactly the way you showed me, and I checked it again before she stepped into the harness. I'm telling you that those carabiners were the proper ones."

"Sssssh, birdie, we believe you," Morrie said. "But it doesn't change the fact that the rigging was sabotaged. This is murder."

"Who had access to the rigging after Quoth checked Zen?" I asked.

"Theoretically, anyone." Morrie pointed to a section of the third-floor gallery seating. "The rigging is operated from the lighting desk, behind the audience on the third gallery. Anyone in the show or audience could have walked past and made the swap while the lighting guy was distracted. Every person in this theater tonight is a suspect."

Quoth buried his head in his hands. "If I'd been more careful, she wouldn't have died."

"You can't blame yourself for this one, birdie." Morrie's voice wavered. "This one is on me."

Morrie turned abruptly and walked over to the side of the stage. I directed Oscar to follow him, and I sat down beside him. "Are you okay?"

"I'm more okay than she is," he answered, wringing his hands in his lap. This was strange for Morrie – he didn't usually show compassion for the victims we investigated. He preferred to look at a murder as a collection of interesting puzzles. But Zen's death had gotten to him.

"You want to tell me what's eating you? Because Quoth is over there freaking out that this is his fault, and it can't be *everyone's* fault."

I meant it as a joke, but Morrie winced, and I wished I could take it back. "All I can think about is that someone got to her before she could tell me what she knew."

"What do you mean?"

"Zen wrote the note. I found a shopping list in her pocket and compared the handwriting." Morrie unfolded the note she left him and read it again. "'Meet me outside the stage door after the show. I have something important to tell you.' What do you think she wanted to tell us? I admit, when I first read this, I thought she was going to confess, but—"

"—but now that she's been murdered," I added, "it reads like Zen knew the identity of the killer."

CHAPTER TWENTY-ONE

With the Shakespeare Festival officially on hold and police swarming over the New New Globe, the Argletonians and visitors to the village had nothing to do except hang about and amuse themselves. Which they did in typical English village style – by overrunning the pub and gossiping endlessly about the murders.

Word got around (thanks, Mrs. Ellis) that we were investigating the murder, and Nevermore Bookshop had never been busier as people picked through our Shakespeare stock and shared endless theories about the murderer's motives. Some believed he was a critic who murdered Zen because she was a terrible Lady Macbeth, while others thought it might've been a jealous lover who wanted her to suffer in true Shakespearean fashion.

I was so busy working the register and fielding outrageous theories that I barely had a chance to think about the case all day. Finally, I couldn't take it any longer and shooed them out of the store with the promise that we'd be around at the pub shortly to continue solving the case over a pint. I went from room to room, ushering the stragglers out the door and slamming it behind them. My feet hurt. My fingers smelled from constantly touching old, inky pages, and I did desperately need a drink.

I was just about to head upstairs for a shower when I heard someone cough in the hall. *Shite, did I forget to bolt the front door?*

"We're closed," I called out. No one answered, but as I came around the corner, I banged straight into a customer.

"Ooof."

"I'm sorry," a familiar voice said. The figure stepped back, underneath one of the lamps I had positioned, and I recognized the bat hoodie. "You're Mina, right?"

"That's me. And you're Bree. I remember your hoodie."

"Thanks." Bree lowered her voice. "Listen, I was at the theater last night. I saw what happened to that poor woman. And I've heard around that you might be investigating these murders on the down-low."

"I wouldn't dream of undermining our constabulary," I said automatically.

"I'm not here to bust your chops. The police couldn't organize a piss up in a brewery." Bree looked over her shoulder. I squinted, but I couldn't see anything there, although I wasn't exactly the best judge. When she turned and spoke again, her voice was even quieter. "I might be able to help."

"How?"

"Okay, so, first, I texted you the images I took of the First Folio. They might come in handy, since I assume the police have it in their possession."

"They actually returned it today," I said. "It belongs to Shelley Rasmussen now, but with Zen gone and the Shakespeare Museum closing, she's decided to loan it to Miles for display in the theater as soon as the restorers have cleaned off the blood. But who knows when I'd actually get to see it, so the photos will help a lot, thank you."

"You're welcome. And…" she paused, shifting her weight from

foot to foot. "This isn't easy for me, and please don't think I'm a freak."

"Bree, I promise, you can't be a bigger freak than me. Just tell me what it is."

"Okay, let's say I happen to be closely acquainted with a… local expert in the Shakespearean period. Someone who you'd very much like to talk to you but for specific reasons, cannot."

She's talking about Zen.

Bree continued. "And this…er, renowned scholar told me to tell you to look at the lily."

"The what?"

"The lily. You must look at the lily. That's all I can tell you." Bree stepped back out of the light, and the shadows fell over her face, obscuring her from my view. "I have no idea what she means, but she seems to think you'll figure it out."

"Wait. How do you know—"

"Good luck, Mina."

"Bree?"

Footsteps rushed away. I shoved my hand into the darkness, but I grabbed only air.

Bree was gone.

Well, that was weird as fuck.

Look at the lily. *What can that possibly mean? And how will it help me uncover a murderer?*

And where exactly did Bree get this strange message?

CHAPTER TWENTY-TWO

"*L*ook at the lily," Morrie mulled over the cryptic message. "It sounds like someone was smoking a little too much of God's holy herb."

"Maybe it's a person?" Quoth suggested. "Someone named Lily?"

"It could be the name of his favorite pornstar for all we know," Heathcliff said. "It's too cryptic to be a clue. We don't have anything to go on, and meanwhile, the police are at the theater, no doubt trying to pin this whole thing on Morrie now that they can't find a fairy in London."

It was true. The police had returned from London without catching their man, and since no one at the theater had reported seeing Puck, they weren't looking at him at the moment. But that didn't mean we were out of trouble. It would be just like them to blame Morrie for sabotaging the rigging. We needed to figure out who the real killer was before he struck again. And the only clue we had to go on was Bree's cryptic message from Zen.

"Are these two crimes even connected?" Heathcliff asked. "We've made that mistake before."

He was right. We had run around in circles during the Banned

Book Club murders because we thought there was one killer when there were really two. But I was certain we were looking at the same hand. These killings were just too dramatic, too…Shakespearean.

"They're connected, I'm sure of it," I said. "Do you remember what I overheard Rasmussen and Delacroix say at the opening night? Rasmussen thought he was 'safe' in Argleton, which implied he *hadn't* been safe in London. And Delacroix wanted to pull the book off public display. Maybe they'd been getting threats? And whatever made them unsafe, whatever it was Zen knew, she paid the price for that knowledge. And until we have another lead, if this Lily can tell us the answer—"

"Oh. Rasmussen had a flower pot on his desk," Quoth said. "I noticed it when I went in to eavesdrop on the police. I can't remember, but it might've been a lily."

"That's got to be it," I said, remembering the pot with the tiny scarlet flower. "I mean, it makes no sense that a plant could give us a clue, but if it's a plant we're looking for, then it's got to be one at the scene of the crime."

"Are you sure we should trust this new friend of yours?" Morrie said. "How do we know she talked to Zen before she died? And why would Zen trust her with this all-important clue? I'm not sure she has all her marbles. I walked in on her in the travel section and she was having an intense argument with herself over whether it was Istanbul or Constantinople. I told her to refer to the song."

"I trust Bree," I said, even though Morrie was right – she seemed a bit mad, and I had no reason whatsoever to trust her apart from the fact that she had great fashion sense. But I couldn't shake the memory of the tremble in her voice when she told me about the lily. "Maybe it's not about the lily itself at all. Maybe there's a key to Rasmussen's secret sex dungeon taped to the bottom of the pot."

"Secret sex dungeon?" Morrie perked up. "We're going."

"*Where* are we going?" Quoth asked.

"To break into the crime scene, of course." Morrie looped his fingers into his kilt. "We'll find the answers, if my name isn't Macbeth—"

"Say that word all you like," Heathcliff snapped. "But I'm not doing a silly dance. If the actors run you out of town for bringing a curse down on their heads, you have only yourself to blame."

I crouched behind the bins in the alley behind Rasmussen's store, squeezed in beside the Napoleon of Crime. He seemed unperturbed with the prospect of breaking yet another law in the name of solving a murder, and was even whistling the tune for 'Istambul not Constantinople' under his breath. I was disappointed in myself that mere days after swearing off crime-solving I was already back in the saddle, but needs must.

We heard an ominous click, followed by a quiet, "Croak."

"Good job, birdie," Morrie whispered. He took my hand and guided me through the back door. We decided breaking in through the back alley would be less obvious than going through the front, especially given how crowded the pub on the green was right now. Quoth had flown in an open window in Delacroix's flat and used his beak to pick the lock from the inside.

Morrie gripped my hand, his fingers tight with excitement. We ducked inside, moving through a messy storage room and underneath the crime scene tape into the main shop. The only light in the place came from the windows looking onto the green, and they were obscured by the high shelves crowded with expensive books.

"I can't see a thing," I said. Good thing I didn't need to see in order to snoop.

I directed Oscar to lead me toward the desk. I felt around

until I found the potted plant on the corner of the desk. The dirt in the pot was bone dry – no one had watered it since Rasmussen's murder. I guess Lawrence wasn't much for flowers.

I heard a faint scraping sound as Morrie picked up the pot and inspected the underside. "No secret sex dungeon key." He sounded disappointed. "No cocaine hidden in the dirt. It looks like a perfectly ordinary…hey, birdie, what kind of flower is this, anyway?"

What do I look like, a botanist? Quoth shot back.

"Wait." I scrambled for my phone. "I have an app…"

I downloaded the app a few weeks ago, because the planters flanking Nevermore's doorway were more weed than plant and I wanted to fix that. But I didn't know what needed pulling out and what should stay behind, and the boys were no help. It was an awesome app – you pointed the phone at a plant and it told you what species it was and whether it was a weed or something pretty and/or useful.

I pointed the camera at the plant and waited for the ding that indicated the app finished its search. My phone read out the information.

"Congratulations, you have *Sprekelia formosissima,* commonly known as the Jacobean lily or Aztec lily. It is a herbaceous perennial bulb that is not a true lily, but the scarlet flowers do resemble lilies, hence their common names. It is native to Mexico and Guatemala, and was brought to England by explorers in 1658…"

"Boring." Morrie yawned. "Does it tell you if you can smoke it? Will it give you hallucinations or make your dick grow horns—"

"No, Morrie, *ssh.*" I stared at the commentary again. Something niggled at me, but I couldn't quite place it. I peered closely at the image on the screen and the wilted plant in front of me…

"…brought to England by explorers in 1658…"

…*1658...*

"That's it," I cried out.

"What's it?"

"Morrie, I sent you those images Bree took of the First Folio. There's one of the first page of *Much Ado About Nothing*, isn't there?"

"I believe so." Morrie tapped away on his phone.

"Hold it up against the flower, and tell me what you see."

"Huh," Morrie held up the screen against the lily. I couldn't quite see the detail in the Folio image, but I knew what he was going to say before he said it.

"It looks identical to Rasmussen's lily here. But I don't see—"

"The Jacobean lily was first discovered and imported to England in 1658." My blood raced in my veins. "But the First Folio was printed in 1623. There is no way that an illustration of *this* flower could be in *that* book unless the author had access to the waters of Meles."

So either the creator of the First Folio is another of Homer's long-lost children, Quoth said. *Or...*

"...or this is what Zen was trying to tell us," I whispered. "This is why she was killed. Rasmussen's First Folio is a fake."

CHAPTER TWENTY-THREE

"*A*re you telling me that the poxy bastard faked that whole book?" Heathcliff said. "And he got it past two expert London authenticators?"

"It's diabolical," Morrie said. "I'm impressed."

"Remember the dude was murdered before you come in your trousers," Heathcliff snapped.

We were back at Nevermore now, crowded into the main room of the bookshop as Morrie and Quoth and I filled Heathcliff in on what we learned.

"A First Folio sold for almost ten million at Christie's," I said. "For Hiram to take it off the market before anyone else could bid, he had to be paying at least that. Even if it took Rasmussen months of work to create it, that's a great ROI."

"I'd love to know how he did it," Morrie said. "Creating fakes is a serious business. Not only does he need to copy the text and illustrations *exactly*, but the ink, the paper, the glue for the bindings, all must be perfect copies of what was used at the time. Any modern ingredients and they'll be caught out immediately. I wish we could ask him—"

Heathcliff punched Morrie in the arm. Morrie stuck his

tongue out, and the whole thing might've devolved into sex on the desk again if Morrie didn't at that moment receive a phone call. He moved off across the room, speaking to the caller in the low, menacing voice he used for his criminal contacts.

"Now that we know it's a fake, it puts a whole new spin on our suspects," Quoth said. "If Hiram knew about the ruse, he'd be livid, and it explains why he wouldn't bother taking the book with him after he hit Rasmussen. And then there's Shelley, with all that cash from a mysterious source…"

"What about Miles?" I pointed out. "We discounted him before because he had no motive, but he *was* in the vicinity at the time of the clobbering. And what if he found out the First Folio was a fake—"

"Oh, he knows the First Folio is a fake all right," Morrie said, dropping his phone on the desk. "My contacts in London have just picked Miles Shackleton up trying to sell it on the black market."

CHAPTER TWENTY-FOUR

Two hours later, we stepped off a train in London and made our way across the city to an abandoned warehouse, where Morrie's 'friends' were keeping Miles.

"Let me handle the interrogation." Morrie smoothed down his hair and tugged on the cuffs of his immaculate suit. My throat went dry – maybe I was a terrible person, but I loved when Morrie got all Crime Lord on us. I was such a sucker for the bad boys, and James Moriarty was the baddest they came. "Quoth, I want you to remain on guard at the window – make sure we're alone. Big man, you lean against the door. Don't say anything, just look mean. Can you handle that?"

"I don't even need acting lessons." Heathcliff cracked his knuckles. "I'm a natural."

Bad boy number two. I pressed my thighs together. *I hope we can get this interrogation over with soon, because I desperately want to take these three home and shag their brains out.*

"Mina, you're my Girl Friday," Morrie said. "I want you by my side. You're going to be his sweet salvation when he needs it most. Let Miles know that all he has to do is cooperate and it will all stop."

"What will stop?" My voice cracked with lust.

"That's for me to know and you to find out." Morrie's words sank right into my toes. I let him take my arm, and we walked into the warehouse together. We were greeted by one of Morrie's 'people' (I don't know what his job was, but I knew he was muscled enough to give Heathcliff a fair fight, so I wasn't going to ask). Reluctantly, I removed Oscar's coat and handed him over. Oscar peered up at the man with his big brown eyes, and the hulking golem of a gangster turned to putty.

"Who's a good boy?" he cooed in a Russian accent, scratching Oscar between the ears. "Do you want a treat? I bet you want a treat. I have *pirozhki* in my office. You want some delicious *pirozhki*? You come with old Viktor and he'll give you all the treats."

Oscar trotted after Viktor, his tail wagging with glee. He didn't mind gangsters either, as long as they had delicious snacks.

"This way." Morrie led the way along a narrow corridor. It smelled like urine and undercooked mince. We stopped in front of a huge steel door. Morrie typed a combination into a keypad, and the door swung open. I stepped into a dim cinderblock room with only a narrow window high on the wall letting in a pale stripe of light. Goosebumps raised on my arms, which had nothing to do with the frigid air.

Morrie flicked on a lamp, which illuminated a man chained to a chair who cringed away in terror. I couldn't see into the darkened corners, but I knew by the smell and the acoustics that the room was bare and cold and lacking in toilet facilities. With a flutter, Quoth flew over my head and disappeared up toward the window ledge to keep a lookout.

The man was Miles Stapleton, and he looked like he'd been locked in here for months, not the few hours it took us to get here from Argleton. I guess Viktor didn't extend his hospitality to his prisoners.

"You're not the police," Miles stammered.

"No, we're not." Morrie pulled a chair out of the darkness and swung his long leg over it, so he straddled it backward. He didn't have to produce a knife to make any threats – just his mere presence, and the looming malice of Heathcliff behind us, made Miles quake. "And that could be good news for you, or bad news, depending on how you answer our questions. And if you give me the information I want, I might hand you over to them with all your fingers intact."

"Mina, I don't know how you got mixed up with this guy, but he's a crook," Miles cried. "Look at what his goons have done to me, and all I tried to do was put on a Shakespeare festival—"

"I'm not taking relationship advice from you, Miles. You stole the First Folio," I said. "*And* you killed Jasper Rasmussen and Zen Monroe."

"No," he cried.

"There's no use denying it," Morrie steepled his fingers. "You had the Folio in your possession, and you were trying to sell it to my friend Viktor. We've identified it as the one belonging to Rasmussen. And we saw you in the square that morning, because you'd just come from murdering an innocent bookseller."

"I took the Folio, okay? But I never hurt Rasmussen. I never even saw him that day! And he wasn't so innocent!"

Ah, now we come to the crux of it. I folded my arms. "I think you'd better explain. Did you know the First Folio was fake?"

"Not at first." Miles put his head in his hands. "When he brought it to me and suggested displaying it in the festival, I did my due diligence. Rasmussen had it authenticated by two Shakespearean authorities in London. He showed me their letters, and I even spoke to one on the phone. I was so excited to have it in the festival – it was guaranteed to bring press attention and new investors to the New New Globe, and Rasmussen agreed to cut me in for half the profits from his tickets if I made him the official festival bookseller. Everything was going perfectly, but then Zen decided to stick her nose in. She paid her two-quid to take a look at the Folio, and she came by immediately and told me that she thought it was a fake, and I shouldn't allow the integrity of the festival to come into disrepute by associating with it."

"How come you didn't tell this to the police?" I asked. If the police had known the folio was fake from the beginning, they might not have spent so much time chasing after Puck. *And Zen might still be alive.*

"How do you know what I did and didn't tell the police?" Miles snapped, straining his chains to lean close to me. Heathcliff was across the room in a moment, looming over him. Miles swallowed. He decided against getting up in my face and in his chains.

"Zen wanted me to tell the police about it, but I told her to keep quiet for now and let me handle it. Rasmussen probably made the fake to sell to someone like Hiram Abernathy, someone who wouldn't look carefully enough to notice the ruse. I didn't care about the book – all I wanted to do was save the festival. As far as I'm concerned, how Hiram spends his money is his business, and if the public gets a kick out of seeing the book, then what's the harm? But if it came out that the First Folio was a fraud, it would throw the whole festival into disrepute and…and…"

"And you'd be ruined," Morrie finished for him. "We know all about where the funds for the New New Globe came from – the mortgage on your house."

"How do you know this?" Miles quaked.

"A little hint," I smiled. "If you want to keep your finances a secret, then don't hire the village gossip to run your festival."

"Yes, yes, fine," Miles snapped. "It's true that I'm in a bit of hot water over the theater. But I thought I could fix things. I got up early and went to speak to Rasmussen. I went down the back alley behind the shops, because I saw Zen in the square and I didn't particularly want to see her. It was unlocked, so I went inside, but as I walked through the storage room, I overheard him having a screaming row with his daughter."

Shelley and Mr. Rasmussen were arguing in the shop? I leaned forward. "What was the argument about? Did you hear?"

"She was yelling that he was going to ruin everything for her," Miles said. "It sounded like a family thing, and I didn't want to intrude, so I snuck out the back of the shop and went to the pub. I thought I'd have one of Richard's famous big breakfasts and clear my head before I talked to him, and I was walking over there when that donkey ran across the square and everyone was up and about. I was eating my sausages and baked beans when the police showed up."

"Wait, you went through the back door?" I asked. "But it was locked."

"It wasn't, I swear. I walked straight outside into the alley."

And the killer locked it after you.

"Can anyone verify you were at the pub?" Morrie asked.

"I thought you'd know that already?" Miles snapped. "Since you know everything."

"Humor us."

"Richard and about five others can confirm we had a lovely conversation about the weather and people who let their fucking donkeys run wild in the streets." Miles looked up at Morrie, his voice wavering. "And that's all I had to do with the whole unfortunate thing until Shelley got the Folio back from the police and loaned it to me to display in the festival. I thought maybe I could sell it to some unsuspecting sod and then claim it was stolen, and I'd get the money I need to fix my finances and my marriage. But then your Viktor hauled me in here to torture me, and here we are."

Morrie leaned in close, his voice dripping with malice. "That's everything you have to tell us?"

"I swear on the ghost of William Shakespeare, I've told you everything I know," Miles sobbed. "Please just hand me over to the police. You aren't going to hurt me, are you?"

*A*fter we extracted Oscar from Viktor's loving embrace, Morrie told him to go back and see Miles and "make sure we had everything." We left Viktor to his work and walked out of the warehouse. Morrie unbuttoned his blazer and loosened his tie. I clutched a heavy book of fake Shakespeare under my arm.

Behind us, I could hear Miles bawling. I didn't want to ask what was going on in there.

"So it wasn't him," Heathcliff said.

"No, it wasn't. But we've got some useful information, and we have the First Folio back." I dropped the book into Heathcliff's arms. "We need to have a talk with Shelley."

CHAPTER TWENTY-FIVE

"Hi, Mina." Shelley placed Max on the ground with a set of colored blocks and settled into a swiveling salon chair. We'd asked her to meet us in the dressing room at the New New Globe, figuring she'd assume it was about the First Folio display. Morrie wanted to lead the interrogation, but Quoth was adamant it was his turn. Personally, I was grateful. Miles' terrified cries still echoed in my ears. "What's up?"

"Hi, Shelley, thank you so much for meeting with us." I settled into a chair opposite her. Quoth sat on the makeup counter, his long legs swinging as he regarded Shelley through a curtain of silken hair. "I know you must be having a horrible time right now, dealing with the funeral arrangements and everything."

"It is awful, but I'm surviving." She used the edge of her sleeve to dab at her eyes. Silently, Quoth passed her a box of tissues. He was even kind to murder suspects.

"As you might've heard, we're looking into your dad's murder."

"And I appreciate it," Shelley said. "I really do. The police aren't doing anything. They're down in London chasing some magician, but that doesn't make any sense. Why would a magician want to hurt my father? I'm positive they'll never catch Dad's real killer."

"I'm inclined to agree," I smiled. "But we have a pretty good track record of solving crime in Argleton. And we've found some new evidence that points toward your father's killer being much closer to home. But we wanted to talk to you before we went to the police because…"

"Because we know what you did," Quoth finished. His body tensed at the words, as if he expected Shelley to strike him.

Shelley's face reddened. "You'd better not be implying that—"

I placed a paper on the table in front of her. "One of the upsides of us investigating a case instead of the police is that we can get into places where they wouldn't legally be able to look. And my friend Morrie found something interesting about you. Your son goes to a super-expensive daycare in Grimdale, and you've had three fancy overseas holidays in the last year and a very nice Prada handbag. That's quite a lifestyle for a single mother on benefits. And the weird thing is, these huge expenditures on your accounts coincide with major items in Rasmussen's collections going up for auction in London."

I placed down a second sheet of paper next to the first, showing the dates where the sales lined up.

Shelley's hands flew to her mouth. "How dare you look into my private accounts. That's none of your business—"

Quoth drew the First Folio from behind his back and dropped it into her lap. "We know it's fake," he said, his voice barely above a whisper. "And you know, too."

Shelley made a choking sound.

"We're duty-bound to hand this information over to the police," I said. "So if you want to get yourself out of a shit ton of trouble, you'd better start talking."

Shelley sighed. "Fine, yes, I knew it was a fake. A lot of Daddy's books are fakes. He has a little workshop in his London flat where he makes them. I think it started as a hobby, just to see if he could. But then he got addicted to the game of pulling the wool over the eyes of his pretentious clients and the stuffy old authenticators. He wanted to teach me how to do it so I could take over the business, but I'm not interested. I told Daddy I'd keep his filthy secret, but he'd better look after me and Max. And he's been true to his word – he's kept his business in London, out of our lives, and we've been able to enjoy a few luxuries because of his generosity. It's a win-win and a victimless crime – it doesn't matter if those books aren't the real thing. They bring people joy. I mean, not even the experts can tell they're fakes, so what's the point? Daddy was never caught, and as long as he kept paying me, I didn't care what he did."

"But then he decided to come to Argleton," I said.

"I told him not to," Shelley said. "I said that we built a good life for ourselves, and I didn't want him bringing his criminal enterprise here, where people gossip and scrutinize every little detail of your life. But he insisted he'd turned over a new leaf. He wasn't going to do any more fakes, just run a legitimate antiquarian business. Hmmmph, another lie. When I heard about Hiram Abernathy and the First Folio, I immediately knew Daddy made a fake. Only this was a high-profile fake with lots of media attention. It was only a matter of time before someone figured it out."

"Someone like Zenzile Monroe," Quoth said. "You killed her because she figured it out. Maybe she even told you, because you were so supportive of the museum."

"I would never hurt Zen!" Shelley slammed her fist on the bench. Concealer bottles rattled and lipsticks rolled over the edge. "She loved Max. She was a good person. No, I went to Dad's shop and threatened to tell the police about the fake First Folio if he didn't withdraw it immediately from the festival and go back to London."

"And then what happened?"

"What do you think happened?" she said. "He told me I was worrying too much, and that he'd got the Folio past the premier

Shakespeare experts in London, and that I wouldn't worry so much if he put ten thousand quid in my account."

Quoth hissed through his teeth.

Shelley continued. "Oh, sure, get all high and mighty. But do you have any idea how expensive nappies are? Ten thousand is a lot of money, and I haven't done anything wrong. If he got caught, it's his own bloody fault. So I left the shop and hurried across the square, getting angrier and angrier that he had gone back on his word to me, and that Zen was suffering because of it, when I ran straight into you." She glared at us both. "You remember, don't you?"

I nodded. "But you disappeared right after that. You could have gone back and killed him."

"What would be the point? Why would I get rid of the gravy train? Sure, I get Dad's business now that he's gone, but I don't know the first thing about running a bookstore, and I can't run around London getting involved in shady fake book deals. I'm a *mother*. I gave this book to Miles because I thought maybe, if people really did believe it's real, it could do some good and save the festival. But if you two spill the beans, then it's the final curtain for the New New Globe."

"You got any proof that you didn't kill your father?"

"I can't prove a negative," Shelley said, "but my dad was alive when I left the shop. Whoever killed him got in after me."

"Which door did you use to enter and leave the shop?" I asked.

"Around the back. Daddy unlocks it in the morning because he smokes his disgusting cigars on the back step." Shelley held up the book. "What should I do with this?"

"Leave it with us for now," I said. "It might come in handy for catching the real killer."

"So I can go?" She gathered her son into her arms. "You're not going to get me locked up?"

"Not right now," Quoth said. "Thank you for talking to us."

Shelley kicked the book across the floor. It skidded to a stop by my feet. She ran out of the room, slamming the stage door behind her. I looked at Quoth, who'd picked up the book and was thumbing through the pages. "She could be lying."

"That's what I thought. But she does have a point – if she was the murderer, why cut off her gravy train? I get being angry at her dad, but if this is over money, I just can't see her clobbering him. And she seemed to genuinely love Zen." I stroked Oscar between the ears. "I know that's not very scientific. If Jo were here, she'd tell me I had to stick to the facts and not get bogged down with statements, because people lie all the time."

"But Jo's not here," Quoth said. "I am."

"Exactly, and no one understands people better than you do. No one spends so much time in the shadows observing. So what do you think?"

"I can't see Shelley hitting her dad over the head with the book," he said. "Something about this crime is so vicious, so *passionate*, it has to be about more than money and fake books."

"I think you're right." I slumped into my hands. "Which means that if it wasn't Miles or Shelley, and we don't think it's Hiram, either, then we're back to square one again."

CHAPTER TWENTY-SIX

"*I* had a little talk with my buddies in London," Morrie said as we wandered across the green toward the pub. We had tickets to the *A Midsummer's Night Dream* performance tonight, but with the ongoing investigation, the New New Globe was closed indefinitely. But Mrs. Ellis had got some of the actors together to recreate key scenes on the tiny stage at the Rose & Wimple, and we wanted to get good seats.

"By 'buddies,' I presume you mean Viktor and other gentlemen of ill-repute?" I grinned.

Morrie inclined his head. "Do you want to hear what they had to say or not?"

"Very much." Quoth ran his hand through his hair, tugging it over his face so he could hide behind it. He didn't even want to go tonight – he said he was tired, but I knew the real reason; he *believed* it was his fault we hadn't caught the killer. He blamed himself for all of Argleton's misfortunes, and when he saw the villagers were hurting, it only convinced him that they'd be better off without him.

I hoped that dragging him along to watch hilarious amateur dramatics with a bunch of drunken villagers would show Quoth that the festival wasn't what mattered in Argleton. Our friends, our family, the way we treat people, our ability to turn the cheek to misfortune and laugh when lady luck spat in our faces – that was what made us who we were. And Quoth was a loved and vital part of village life. No one thought him as evil and unworthy as he believed himself to be.

I could tell that he blamed himself for our failure to catch the killer – he wanted so badly to give the town back the festival, but so far all we'd done was uncover deeper and deeper layers of corruption. I didn't know what to say to convince him that just because we hadn't solved the case, and just because he'd hurt people when he was under Dracula's influence, it didn't mean that my kind, wonderful birdie was in any way unworthy.

But I'm no Brene Brown or Socrates. I was just a girl who worked in a bookshop and loved three imperfect but wonderful men. I didn't know how to help him, except by being beside him, by telling him always that I loved him because of who he was, not for what he did. I squeezed Quoth's hand as Morrie told us what he'd uncovered.

"It turns out that in the seedy criminal underbelly of London, our Mr. Rasmussen had quite the reputation as a document forger. He's been pulling this con on unsuspecting clients for years – forging old books to sell for exorbitant prices. Often, he deliberately targeted specific collectors, dangled their favorite authors in front of them, then alluded that he might offer the book to a university or invent other interested parties to drive up the price. The collectors were so anxious to have the item that they weren't as thorough with provenance as they might usually be, and if they later uncovered the truth, they were too embarrassed to report the crime."

"And he was trying to pull this trick on Hiram Abernathy with the First Folio," Heathcliff said. My gothic antihero walked with a spring in his step. Everything was coming up Heathcliff tonight –

we were close to alcohol, and with the festival shut down, the shop was once again empty of customers.

"Abernathy is the perfect mark – he's rich as Croesus, and he knows next to nothing about the objects he purchases." Morrie tapped his chin. "But I don't think that's what was happening here. If he wanted to sell the book to Abernathy, why put it into the festival at all? Why draw unwanted attention from media and Shakespeare scholars? Something doesn't add up here."

"If we're going to add it up, can we do it near the bar?" Heathcliff tugged on Morrie's sleeve.

"I think we need to take another look at Hiram," Quoth said as we entered the Rose & Wimple. "He's at a table in the corner with his wife, and they're sharing a piece of cake with two candles. How *sweet*. Maybe we should corner him when he goes to the bathroom, try to get the truth out of him."

"Or *maybe*, since it was his wife's birthday yesterday, we should leave them to have a fun night, and we should do the same," I said. *This isn't what tonight is supposed to be. We're trying to cheer Quoth up, not make him obsess even more.* "Come on, I asked Mrs. Ellis to save us a booth near the stage—"

"Do you think Hiram found out the folio was fake?" Quoth went on. I didn't think he even heard me. "We saw he's terrified of his wife. What if *she* found out and sent him for revenge for trying to deceive her? He did have that mysterious red stain on his shirt—"

"But the timing doesn't work," I pointed out as we sat down. "We saw Hiram with his bloodstained shirt before Miles overheard the fight between Shelley and her dad, and he was an ass at the time—"

"Hark," a voice cried from across the table. My chest tightened as I realized our party had been crashed by a mysterious figure, who was currently having his ear talked off by Mrs. Ellis. Although, as I leaned forward and took in his silhouette and comically fake mustache, he was actually painfully familiar.

Surely he wouldn't come back, not after we told him how dangerous it was for him now...

"What are you doing here, Puck?" I hissed as Mrs. Ellis got up to smear Heathcliff, Morrie, and Quoth with kisses.

Puck waved a sickly-smelling flower under my nose. "A suspect found I none, on whose eyes I might approve, this flower's force in stirring love..."

I swiped at the flower, but he held it out of my reach. "Thanks for the offer of help, but you can't be here. If Hayes sees you in that ridiculous mustache, he'll recognize you immediately. And you can't go around making people fall in love to solve murders. That's not how things work—"

In response, Puck held up the flower and blew on it, just as Mrs. Ellis sank into the seat beside him. As the delicate blossom blew over her face, she stiffened, her body trembling so hard the table shook.

"Puck, what have you done?"

"Upon thy eyes I throw all the power this charm doth owe," he shot back.

"No, you silly goblin, Mrs. Ellis isn't a suspect. Remove the spell *this instant* or by Isis, I'll—"

"Right, here's the first round." Heathcliff slid into the chair beside me, a tray of drinks in his hands. He started slamming glasses on the table. "The first of many if I'm forced to sit through three hours of terrible Shakespeare with you two cackling beside me. Mina, I got you a G&T, and another for Mabel—"

As he slid her drink in front of her, Mrs. Ellis looked up. Her body trembled as she stared deep into his anthracite eyes. "H-H-Heathcliff?"

"That's my name," Heathcliff held up his drink in a half-hearted attempt to toast her. "Have you forgotten? Are you going senile, or are you just half-cut? I hope you didn't start drinking without us, because I'll be catching up, old lady—"

"What light, beyond the window breaks?" She lunged across the table. "I am the east, and Heathcliff is my sun."

Heathcliff yelped as she knocked the drink from his hands, cupped his face, and planted a long, passionate kiss on his lips. He tried to wriggle away, but she was a woman possessed.

"Get off me, you crazy woman, you dissembling harlot." Heathcliff managed to tear her face from his. This close, I could see Mrs. Ellis' eyes glazed over, her lips pouted with need. "I do desire that we be better strangers."

"You have such a February face," Mrs. Ellis cooed as she pinched his cheeks and shoved his head against her breast. "So full of frost, of storm and cloudiness. Let me kiss away your pain, my love. Let me make tender love to you—"

"Save me!" Heathcliff ducked under her arm and bolted from the table. Mrs. Ellis took off after him, crashing through tables and vaulting other diners in her quest to make Heathcliff hers.

"She's surprisingly sprightly for an old woman," Morrie said.

"Well, when you have your eye on a prize," Quoth added.

The pair of them laughed as they watched Mrs. Ellis chase Heathcliff all over the pub. But I couldn't see the humor in it. Puck had made her fall in love against her will, and I couldn't blame anyone for loving wild and beautiful Heathcliff so.

I kept coming back to that rapt expression on her face when the spell hit her – an expression of pure devotion.

An expression I'd seen before.

And suddenly, the missing pieces of the puzzle clicked into place.

"I've got it," I said. "Someone has been lying to us. I know who the killer is."

CHAPTER TWENTY-SEVEN

"So what's the plan?" Heathcliff said as we gathered around his desk. We ducked out of the pub last night after Richard jumped on stage in a donkey costume and Hiram Abernathy fainted from fright, and I sent Quoth and Morrie off to make some arrangements. It was now teatime the next day, and I was ready to spring our trap.

"We're going to trick the killer into confessing," I said. "When they walk through the door, Puck's going to hit them with a love spell. They'll fall in love with Morrie and confess their wickedest sins, which Morrie will record on his phone and send to Hayes. Simple."

"Not simple." Heathcliff shuddered, no doubt remembering his own experience of being in the path of a love potion. "You forget that you've got a reputation in this town. Let's play this out, shall we? The killer has so far gotten away with not one, but *two* murders. Then out of the blue, the village amateur sleuth invites them around to the bookshop, where multiple murderers have been apprehended, for a potluck dinner. You don't think that's the least bit suspicious?"

"Ah, but you didn't count on my wit and cunning," I said. "I sent the invite anonymously, and it was an offer they couldn't refuse. *And* I didn't invite them to the bookshop. We're meeting on the stage at the New New Globe."

"Of course we bloody are," Heathcliff sighed.

"It's only appropriate this tale of love and betrayal and murder end on Shakespeare's stage." Morrie propped his leg up on the table and slashed his sword through the air.

"Put that thing away, you'll put someone's eye out," Heathcliff growled.

"I'm hurt." Morrie pouted as he pretended to wipe his tears on the hem of his kilt, lifting it further up his leg to give a tantalizing glimpse of toned thigh.

"I was talking about your *other* sword."

"We should get going." Quoth gave Morrie a light shove toward the door. "We don't want to be late."

I reached across to my birdie and squeezed his hand. *This is it. This is our chance to catch the crook.* I hoped that whatever happened tonight, Quoth found the peace and acceptance that he so craved, but I had a bad feeling that if he was looking for redemption in our killer, he was pecking at the wrong tree.

We stepped out of the shop and made our way across the green, trying to look as if we were going about normal business and not about to confront a dangerous killer. I decided to leave Oscar out of tonight's shenanigans. He was at Mum's being spoiled rotten with dog treats. I squeezed Quoth's arm extra tight. Tonight, he was my eyes.

When we arrived at the New New Globe, all was in darkness. We went around the back and found the stage door open, exactly as I directed Mrs. Ellis. We crept inside and made our way through props and costumes to stand on the huge, darkened stage. The air sparkled with magical tension. I couldn't see or hear him, but Puck was in the house with his love-in-idleness flower at the ready.

"Do you see anything?" I asked. "Is he here yet?"

"Give me a moment." Morrie was up in the galleries. He ducked into the lighting box and a moment later, a bright spotlight swung across the stage and illuminated a willowy figure.

"Hello, Mr. Delacroix," I said. "Just the person we wanted to see."

CHAPTER TWENTY-EIGHT

"*You.*" Lawerence Delacroix jumped at my voice. "The meddling girl from the bookshop. I should have guessed you were the one who left me that note."

"Yes," I said. "You should have. But you were too blinded by your love, isn't that right? When you got my note saying that Zen had love notes Rasmussen wrote to you, and that you should come to the theater if you wanted to read them, you couldn't resist, could you?"

Lawrence Delacroix growled low in his throat. I pressed on, taking strength from Quoth's steady hand in mine.

"You were in love with Jasper Rasmussen, weren't you?" I asked. "I remember how your voice trembled and tears streaked your face when you saw him lying dead behind his desk. You weren't his flatmate, you were his secret lover, hidden away above his shop where no one could find out. He refused to declare your relationship to the world. Even now, he haunts you, because you loved him even as you watched the life drain from him. You suffer from the deepest, most harrowing kind of unrequited love. And that's why you killed him."

"If you think you're going to get me talking like they do in the

STEFFANIE HOLMES

movies, then you're even sillier than I realized." Lawrence turned on his heel. "Goodnight, Mina—"

"Halt, villain," Puck cried, appearing from thin air in front of Lawrence.

Lawerence froze. "B-b-but how did you do that? You're supposed to be in London—"

"It's magic." Puck lunged for Lawrence, spreading the flower's juice under his eyes before disappearing again in a cloud of fairy dust. Morrie stepped forward, his phone ready to record Lawrence's confession. But Lawrence was so freaked out from seeing Puck's magic that he staggered backward. His foot caught on a loose cable and he toppled over the edge of the stage.

"No!" Quoth cried. He moved so fast I didn't even feel him leave my side, but a moment later he appeared at the stage steps, carrying a dazed Lawrence in his arms.

"My hero," Lawerence cooed, his voice choked with passion as he peered up at his true love.

Right into Quoth's fire-ringed eyes.

CHAPTER TWENTY-NINE

Quoth set Lawrence back on the stage, directly under the spotlight. "No one else is dying on my watch."

"My love." Lawrence fell at Quoth's feet, wrapping his arms around his legs and kissing the tips of his shoes. "You saved me. I'm so happy."

"Oh, no," Morrie whispered. "He's fallen for Quoth instead of me."

"Um…" Quoth sounded terrified.

Heathcliff moaned. "This is a disaster."

"No, it's not," I called out. "Quoth, Lawrence is in love with you. Get him talking."

"Oh, um, sure." Quoth turned to Lawerence and patted him on the head like a dog. "So, Lawrence, um, my darling, I'm so happy we can be together now that you got rid of that pesky Jasper Rasmussen."

Quoth's voice cracked with nerves. He didn't have Morrie's quick tongue, and he was so terrified of getting this wrong…but Puck's flower must be more potent than we thought, because Lawrence clung to Quoth's cartoon supervillain words, sobbing with gratitude.

"You have it all wrong, my love," Lawrence cried, tightening his grip on Quoth. "I didn't mean to kill Jasper! I merely went downstairs to talk to him. Already that morning we had his daughter and that Zenzile woman confronting him about the book, and I was terrified that they would go to the police and ruin everything for us."

"Tell me what happened." Quoth kept stroking Lawrence's hair. "Are you saying you knew the book was a fake?"

"Of course I knew. I helped Jasper make it, and many other fakes we've sold over the years. Jasper Rasmussen is that rare kind of criminal who didn't do it for profit. He was in it for the intellectual challenge, the thrill of pulling the wool over the eyes of an unsuspecting mark."

"What did I tell you?" Morrie nudged me. "Game recognizes game."

"Okay, but then why put the First Folio under public scrutiny?" Quoth flicked his hair from his eyes as Lawrence covered his hands in loud kisses. "Why not simply sell it to Abernathy?"

"I wanted him to get rid of it, but he wouldn't listen," Lawrence sniffed. "Jasper was tired of fooling his simpleton clients. They were no longer a challenge for him. He wanted notoriety. He wanted to advertise himself as the most accomplished forger of our age. And what better way to do this than to forge the most famous writer who ever lived, and get the fake First Folio on the front page of every paper in the country."

"Ah," Morrie whispered. "I understand now. Rasmussen was using the publicity to advertise his forgery services to other criminals. Many in my circle have pulled similar stunts."

"Not you, though?" Heathcliff said with a sardonic lilt in his voice.

"Oh, no, I wouldn't *dream* of it."

"Sssssh," I whispered, jabbing my finger at Morrie's phone. He held it out to capture the confession, but if we talked too close to it all Hayes and Wilson would hear is Morrie and Heathcliff's obscene flirting.

"—the actual forgery was easy to accomplish," Lawrence was saying. "Many educational institutions have their First Folios available as digital scans. We used them as templates, and Jasper has years of experience creating a perfect facsimile of the rag paper used during this period. It took some experimenting to get the inks exactly right, and the workshop stank for weeks after he made the red goatskin binding."

"But you made one critical mistake," Quoth said. "You used illustrations of the Jacobean lily for the title illustration in *Much Ado About Nothing* – a lily that couldn't possibly be drawn when the First Folio was printed."

"No, no, my love. We did that on purpose," Lawrence said. "Jasper always included one anachronism in his forgeries, one obvious clue staring a collector or authenticator in the face. That was part of the game for him, wondering when they would spot it. But people are so excited to have found a treasure, a never-before-seen book that promises untold wonder and riches, that they don't see what's right in front of them."

"Zen Monroe did," I snarled.

"Yes." Lawrence sounded dazed. He turned his head briefly toward us before focusing back on Quoth. "She came to the shop the day before my Jasper died, paid her two pounds to look at the book, and the moment her eyes fell on the illustration I knew she figured it out. I was terrified for Jasper. I knew she'd go straight to the authorities, and I didn't want him to get in trouble. That morning, when I saw her walking across the square towards the shop, I knew she was coming to confront him. I went downstairs to warn him, and my Jasper…he *laughed* at me. He said I was worried about nothing, and that if two Shakespeare experts in London couldn't spot a fake, then a washed-up academic had no chance. And I couldn't help myself, I was trying to save his life and he treated me like…like *nothing*. All the feelings I've been holding in for months came rushing out of me. I don't know what I said but it must have been so cruel, so shocking, because he was struck dumb by me. I told him I was done pretending to be his apprentice. I wanted to be his partner, in business and in life."

"And he rejected you," Quoth said, his voice soothing.

Lawrence sniffed. "He said that he would never do that, and I either accepted my place in his life or he'd find someone else. As if our love could be tossed away like an old paperback! A red mist descended over me. I didn't even know what I was doing. One moment, he stared down at me, telling me that I'd need to move out of the shop by the end of the week, and the next he'd crumpled to the floor and I gripped the bloodstained book in my hands."

A chill ran down my spine as I listened to him recall the gruesome scene. I couldn't imagine it – I loved Quoth, Morrie, and Heathcliff with a love that was more than love, and the idea that I could be so angry that I'd hit them over the head with a book…I knew then that the love Lawrence felt wasn't love as I knew it, it was the kind of twisted, corrupted love, like that which festered between Macbeth and Lady Macbeth, the kind of love that always ended in a tragedy worthy of Shakespeare.

"How could he be dead?" Lawrence sobbed. "I loved him so, as I love you now, my beautiful dark prince."

No, you didn't. You don't understand what real love is.

Love was what tethered me to the spot, watching a murderer kiss my beloved Quoth. Love was the only thing that kept me from springing forward to kick Lawrence's head in with my trusty cherry-red Docs, and judging by the way Heathcliff trembled beside me, love was all that held his fury back, too.

As much as we wanted to run in and tear that murderer off him, Quoth *needed* this. He needed to be the one to drag the confession out of Lawrence. And he was doing it! We almost had everything...

"Please, my love, my beautiful, you must say you forgive me. You must soothe away this pain that haunts me."

Quoth choked as Lawrence squeezed his chest, lifting his shirt to kiss the skin above his belly button. "Um, hold on just a minute, my darling. Could you tell me more about what happened after this...er, terrible tragedy?"

"Yes, yes," Lawrence grasped Quoth's coat. "I was very clever, just as Jasper taught me. I waited until Zenzile knocked on the door and left in a huff, and then I locked the back door and unlocked the front and rearranged the coffee mugs so it looked as if Jasper was expecting someone. I went back upstairs and planned to walk down and discover him and call the police, when I heard your friends enter the shop. I hid in my bed and convinced everyone I'd been sound asleep – I *was* a Shake-spearean actor in college, you know."

"Oh yes," Heathcliff huffed. "We know."

"I thought that after his gruesome death, Zenzile would let his memory rest, but no, she wanted to tell the world what she knew. I was watching her carefully, and I saw her put the note on Morrie's mirror. She planned to destroy the legacy of my great love, and I couldn't have it." Lawrence shuddered in Quoth's arms.

"But you're the one who destroyed his actual body—" Heath-cliff yelped as I clamped my hand over his mouth. We needed to get Lawrence's words on the recording.

"I tampered with her harness so she would fall," Lawrence sniffed. "I know it was horrid to witness, my love, but you must understand why it was necessary. You understand that I did what I had to do to keep Jasper's memory safe, and now I'll do what must be done so that we can be together."

Lawrence whipped out an object from his belt and pointed it

directly at Morrie. I could only see the outline of it, but I knew from the strangled sound Heathcliff made that it was a gun.

"I know they are your friends, but we'll run away together and make new friends. They have to go."

CHAPTER THIRTY

*B*y *Isis, this isn't good.*

"Hey, Lawrence, let's not get carried away," Morrie said. His voice was calm. Too calm. There was none of that usual Morrie swagger.

My master criminal was afraid.

"Puck, where are you?" I whispered. "We could use some magic right about now."

It figures the capricious fairy chooses this exact moment *to go completely silent.*

Heathcliff growled low in his throat, the sound utterly terrifying. Lawrence swallowed, but he cocked the trigger and kept the gun trained on Morrie's face. Heathcliff could snap Lawrence like a twig, but he wouldn't be fast enough to stop Lawrence shooting.

"I have to do it, don't you see?" Lawrence's voice trembled. "It's the only way Allan and I will be free. We'll go far, far away from this place and start over again. Maybe we'll join a theater and he could make the sets and I'll play Titus Andronicus once more."

"Sure, Lawrence," Quoth said, his voice strong and calm. "That sounds like an amazing life."

"But we can't be truly free, my love, because they know my secret." Lawrence gritted his teeth. His arm wobbled. "We must kill your friends."

"Sure, of course." Quoth wrapped his arm around Lawrence's bicep. I thought he might try to pull his arm down so the gun pointed away from Morrie, but he merely stroked Lawrence's skin. "You're right. We *do* need to kill them."

"What?" Heathcliff spluttered.

"But first," Quoth slid his hand down to cup Lawrence's wrist, the movement so soft and gentle it made my chest ache, "I wondered if you would do me the honor of this dance?"

Blood pounded in my ears. Even though I trusted Quoth, I couldn't help but remember the only time I heard him lie. I was back in the art gallery, with Quoth's fangs sinking into my flesh, and my beautiful birdie wanted to hurt me, to take me away from everything I loved.

But Quoth only did that because he wasn't himself, because he'd been taken over by Dracula's power. It wasn't *Quoth* who wanted to do those awful things. It was Dracula, working through Quoth, using his body like a puppet to get to me.

The trauma lived in my skin. My whole body trembled as the memory assailed me, but I closed my eyes and I focused on the sweetness in Quoth's voice, and I knew exactly what he was trying to do.

"You want to dance?" Lawrence's voice hushed. "With me?"

"Of course," Quoth said. "I understand why you've been hurting so much. Jasper wouldn't acknowledge your love in public. He wanted you to be his in secret, and you could never dance together the way you wanted to. And I want to show you that you're worth loving, and you're worth dancing with. I don't want to hide our feelings in front of this audience of doomed booksellers. I want to proclaim our love to the world. So I ask you again, may I have this dance?"

As if by magic, a haunting waltz wafted through the empty theater. *Puck, you bastard.*

Lawrence let out a quiet gasp. I opened my eyes just in time to see him drop the gun on the floor and knit his fingers in Quoth's.

Heathcliff surged forward to grab the gun, but I threw my hand across my chest and held him back. Lawrence was still close, and this couldn't come down to a struggle over a loaded weapon. *Please, let Quoth work his magic.*

Quoth danced across the stage with Lawrence, their eyes locked. Raven hair flared out around them. I held my breath. Beside me, Morrie's fingers laced in mine. Quoth dipped Lawrence, dancing his lips close to Lawrence's neck, almost but not quite a kiss.

The music reached a crescendo. Quoth slid back on his feet, bowing deeply as he looked up at his partner.

"That was amazing, my love. Now, for our grand finale." Lawrence bent and picked up the gun, whipping it around and aiming it at Morrie's head.

Quoth stomped his foot. Right on the lever that operated the stage trapdoor.

BOOM.

SPROING.

It all happened in slow motion…

…the gunshot echoed through the empty theater…

…the trapdoor popped open directly beneath Lawrence's feet…

…the spotlight swung…

…the shadows danced around me as my world receded into two flame-ringed eyes…

…Lawrence screamed as he toppled into the hole, followed by a sickening crunch and an even more sickening silence…

The gun skidded across the stage. The shot went wide, thanks to Quoth. Heathcliff lunged for the gun. Meanwhile, Morrie rushed to the trapdoor and peered into the gloom.

"I don't think he's dead, more's the pity. He's unconscious, though, and his leg looks broken."

I had someone more important to worry about. I ran to Quoth and swept him into my arms, burying my face into his neck. "You did it. You saved us."

"I did, didn't I?" Quoth kissed my hair. "I was so scared, Mina. I was so terrified when he started waving that gun around that I'd lose you. And I didn't want you to think that I had betrayed you again—"

"Don't be silly. The moment you asked him to dance, I figured out what you were planning." I kissed him, long and deep, because for a moment when that gun went off I didn't know if he was dead or alive, and I never wanted to lose him. "Oh, Quoth, you can't keep blaming yourself for what happened. Don't you see? What you did today, how you saved all of us, *that's* the Quoth we know and love, and you proved yourself to be so much stronger than what Dracula made you into."

"I love you, Mina." He nuzzled my cheek.

"I love you, you grim, ghastly, gaunt and ominous bird of yore," I whispered back.

As I held him, the tiniest bit of tension in his shoulders released. Quoth had finally started to let go of the shame that wrapped around his heart. His healing wasn't over, but it had begun, and that was the important thing.

I won't lose him to the darkness.

"Right, Hayes is on his way." Morrie came over to us, his fingers tapping away on his phone. He slid the device into his jacket pocket, and his fierce grey eyes met mine. His arms wrapped around both of us. "Good job, birdie."

"You saved Morrie's face from becoming a Picasso painting." Heathcliff crushed the three of us against his barrel chest, his breathing labored. I knew he was thinking about what would've happened if Lawrence Delacroix's shot had hit its target.

Heathcliff and Morrie had known Quoth for much longer than me. They've been by his side through his early days as a shapeshifting raven boy, and they gave him the space and the fancy to find his own place in the world. Morrie gifted him paints. Heathcliff threw every book about art at him (often literally). They stoked his beautiful, beguiling heart to grow, to strive, and to love.

They may have had their own simmering attraction to deal with, but they still love Quoth with the fierceness that only Heathcliff Earnshaw and James Moriarty were capable of.

Quoth sank into our embrace, and as he lowered his head to mine to kiss me again, I felt another piece of his sadness break away and scatter itself to the wind.

"Oooh, group hug." Puck bounded over.

"GO AWAY," we yelled in unison.

Puck stuck out his lower lip. "Canst I at least turn one of you into a walrus?"

"I think you've done enough," Heathcliff snarled.

Puck sighed. "Fair is foul, and foul is fair. So, good night unto you all. Give me your hands, if we be friends. And Robin shall restore amends."

Reluctantly, I stuck my hand out. Morrie and Quoth followed. Heathcliff growled, but eventually he shoved his beefy fist under Puck's nose. Puck kissed each of our hands. When his lips touched my wrist, a sparkle of magic surged through my body. I didn't know what he was doing, but it felt great.

Puck snapped his fingers and disappeared into a shower of sparkles. The magic hummed in my veins long after he departed.

"Do you think that's the last we've seen of him?" I asked.

Heathcliff snorted. "Puck is attracted to mischief like a moth to a flame, and you, Mina Wilde, you are mischief walking. He'll be back, mark my words."

Laughing, I held my three loves close, breathing their mingled scents of spicy peat moss and lavender and vanilla and chocolate and fresh-cut grass. And I thought how fitting it was that we'd finished this story of love and death and betrayal where all great stories begin – on the stage…

I guess Shakespeare was right, after all – All's well that ends well…

No. I mustn't think that. There will be another murder, another village fiasco, another tragedy, another one of Mum's get-rich-quick-schemes, and many many more days to be in love with these three remarkable men.

CHAPTER THIRTY-ONE

"*I*n recognition of his bravery and quick-thinking in apprehending the killer, who will be rotting in Her Majesty's prison for a good long time, we'd like to award our good friend Allan Poe – who some of us affectionately know as Quoth – with the key to the village."

I cheered so loud my voice went hoarse as Richard held out a glittering gold key. Quoth hid his face behind a curtain of silken hair as he shuffled onto the stage at the pub to accept his award. Everyone in the room stood up and clapped.

And I do mean *everyone*. The whole village had shown up. Even Hiram and Dolores Abernathy were here, dressed in their Texas chic and clapping along. (Hiram sheepishly explained to us that he was sneaking around to get himself some British baking, and the stain on his shirt was blood from when he cut his fingers picking the lock his wife put on his hotel room door.) Jo and Fiona tried to start a mosh pit. Mrs. Ellis put her fingers in her mouth and let out an ear-piercing whistle. (I'd forgotten about the power of that whistle – she used to use it to break up fights on the playground. It wouldn't surprise me if an entire generation of Argleton school children would need hearing aids later in life.)

Mrs. Ellis sat down at our table and patted Heathcliff's knee. He winced – even though Puck reversed the spell, he was still traumatised by his brief period as the object of her desires. She leaned in close with a glint in her eye and whispered, "If I were in my virile youth, you never would have got away, young man."

Heathcliff swallowed.

I turned my attention back to the stage. Quoth had been shaking so bad with nerves before he got on stage, I was afraid he'd drop the key. But he surprised me by flinging his hair out of his face and beaming into the crowd. My heart nearly broke with pride, but it was nothing compared with the newfound peace he had in himself.

"Would you like to say a few words, Quoth?" asked Richard.

Quoth shook his head so ferociously that his hair flicked Richard across the face.

He's still the same Quoth, though.

"Fine, fine. Our Allan is a man of actions, not words. But I hope you'll all join us for a few celebration drinks." Richard started to walk off stage, but turned back as something occurred to him. "And Allan, your tab is on the house tonight."

"Excellent." Morrie rubbed his hands together. "I'm off to the bar to get Richard to make four of his most ridiculous and expensive cocktails. For our hero Allan, of course."

Morrie ran off just as Quoth shuffled off stage and into my arms. I laughed into his silken hair. "Who's going to tell Morrie that the most expensive cocktail Richard knows how to make is a Taming of the Shrewdriver?"

"Not me," Quoth said with a chuckle. It sounded so good to hear him laugh again.

"I'll have two," Heathcliff added. He clapped Quoth on the shoulder so hard he ground bones.

We settled into a table in the middle of the room, and all night the villagers stopped by to congratulate Quoth. At least three people whipped out their phones to show him pictures of his paintings on the walls in the homes. Jo and Fiona returned from the Cotswolds today, and they stopped by especially to smother Quoth in red lipstick kisses. "I missed talking art and weird horror films with you, friend," Jo said as she downed the rest of my Shrewdriver. "Fiona likes rom coms. Blah."

Quoth couldn't stop beaming.

Morrie ended up behind the bar, pouring all kinds of cocktails and surreptitiously putting them on Quoth's tab while Richard wasn't looking. Heathcliff got completely smashed and ended up singing Barbara Streisand songs on the karaoke machine with all the old biddies. All our favorite people showed up to honor Quoth, except…I cast my eyes around the room, which was kind of useless because I was quite literally blind drunk, but still…

…where is she?

"I wonder where Mum is tonight?" I asked Morrie as he finally quit the bar and plopped something fruity and gin-filled in front of me. "I thought she'd love to see one of my boyfriends being honored as an upstanding citizen."

Morrie grinned. "You'll laugh when I tell you."

"I'm not sure I will." My gin-soaked stomach lurched. "Where is she?"

"You know how she had that business predicting when certain authors would die? Well, one of them did. Stella Mey popped her clogs this morning and all these nut jobs have stormed Sotheby's in London, demanding a million quid apiece for their battered old paperbacks. One of them snitched about your mother's Tiktok so now the police are questioning Helen Wilde down at the station as a possible suspect. They think she might've been planning to knock off more authors to improve her bottom line. Good thing you haven't published your novel yet, or you might've been next."

*A*s Morrie and I dragged a singing Heathcliff up the steps of Nevermore Bookshop, Quoth ran ahead to unlock the door. We lurched drunkenly over the threshold and collapsed in a heap on the rug. Grimalkin leaped down from the poetry shelf and climbed over Heathcliff to bat at Quoth's shiny new key.

"Meow?"

"Oh no, you don't. That's not a toy." Quoth whipped it away from her. "And I don't want to see any teeth marks in it, either. This isn't like my marshmallow egg you stole – there's no gooey chocolate inside."

"Meow." Grimalkin huffed. She turned and presented her ass to us, just to show that she couldn't care less about the chocolate-less key.

Yup. That's my grandmother.

"Aarf!" Oscar bounded around the corner, skidding across the floorboards in his haste to see me. I nuzzled his face, earning a face full of wet dog kisses.

"I'm sorry boy, I know you love going to the pub, but I had… hic…my boys looking after me and…hic…" I covered my mouth as I lurched on my side. "…I'm really toasted."

"You're not the only one. We'd better get this fool to bed," Morrie huffed. Heathcliff sagged against his shoulder, snoring loudly. Quoth slid his arm under Heathcliff's other shoulder and helped Morrie drag his dead weight toward the stairs.

"I'll take Oscar out for a bathroom break and I'll see you up there," I called.

"Don't be too long," Morrie called back. "I have plans for drunken, uninhibited Mina."

Grinning, I clipped on Oscar's lead and headed out the back door. We'd left all the lamps on, knowing that we'd likely be legless when we got home and I'd need the light. Grimalkin trotted after us, telling me in loud, plaintive yowls *exactly* what she thought about us having fun without her.

"Look, I'm sorry we didn't invite you, but I can't exactly explain to the villagers why my grandmother looks ten years older than me and is licking cream from a saucer, so—Bree?"

I stopped in surprise as my new friend stepped in front of the glittering lamps. I felt momentarily frightened that she'd caught me talking to my cat, but then I remembered the weird conversations she had with thin air and figured I was probably safe from further scrutiny.

"Hi, Mina, I'm so sorry for giving you a fright. I was walking past and the door was open so I thought I'd see if you were around and not too pissed..." she peered at me. "It looks like that ship has sailed."

"It's cool to see you again." I leaned against the doorframe, which was currently the only thing keeping me upright. "What are you doing here?"

"I heard you and your boyfriend solved the murder of that dead bookstore dude," Bree said. "I came by to say congrats. I was going to the ceremony at the pub, but I got...er, held up on some things."

She said this as she threw a withering look over her shoulder. My head swam. I didn't know what to make of her, but I was too drunk to judge.

"Oh, thank you. I mean, it was really Quoth who saved the day. But we wouldn't have gotten there without your help. We figured out that clue you gave us and that led us right to the killer."

"Cool." Bree shifted on her feet. "So..."

I wanted to ask her to stay and hang out, but I was focusing too hard on remaining upright.

Bree looked over her other shoulder, and it might've been my drunken state, but I swear I heard her say, "...yeah, yeah, I'm getting to it."

"What…hic…was that?" I said.

"Oh, nothing." Bree fished around in her bag. "So, um, I saw this in Grimdale, and I thought Oscar would like it."

She placed something in my hand. I angled the nearest light and brought it right under my nose so I could see it was a bandana covered in little dancing skeletons.

"The skeletons glow in the dark," Bree grinned.

"I love it, and so does Oscar. Thank you so much." I tied the bandana around Oscar's collar and got him to stand up so Bree could see. "Say, do you want to come upstairs for a drink?"

"Haven't you been drinking at the pub all night?" she asked. "I wouldn't want to keep you up if you just want to go to bed—"

"Nonsense." I waved my hand, aware of just how much Heathcliff Earnshaw was rubbing off on me. "I work in the book industry. There's always a reason to drink."

"*T*his is a pretty cool place." Bree kicked off her boots and stretched her feet out in front of the fire. I'd had to ask her to light it because I was drunk and useless and the guys had all passed out in our big bed.

"It's a little cramped with four of us living here, but we make it work." I dumped a mountain of Heathcliff's books and Quoth's art supplies off the chair and settled in opposite Bree. Something round and hard dug into my ass. I reached beneath me and pulled out a bottle of Lagavulin, which I held out to Bree. "Will this do?"

"Yes, please." Bree took the bottle and poured us both a dram. "So, can I ask, are you and those three guys all, like…together?"

"Yes." I might not have answered so truthfully if I wasn't so drunk. I sipped my whisky. I couldn't even taste it. Not a great sign. "We used to be discreet about it because, you know, village life. But now we don't care. Let people talk. Now that I'm blind I can't see their disapproving faces so…"

She leaned forward, her voice quivering with interest. "What's it like having three boyfriends?"

"Why do you want to know?" I teased. "Want to give it a go yourself?"

Bree leaped out of her chair like someone had pinched her. "Y-y-y...no, yes. I don't know. There are three guys in my life, but they're more annoying than anything. Plus, it's complicated."

"It's always complicated. You want to tell me about them?"

"Yes, but I'm working up to it."

"That's cool," I slurred. "Tell me about something else, like... how did you know about the lily? Zen told you, didn't she? She was acting all weird when we saw her in the quad."

"Yeah. But that wasn't about the fake. She'd just seen Lawrence hit Rasmussen. He threatened her – no doubt told her that he knew dangerous people in the criminal book forging world, and they'd go after her or the people she loved if she talked. So she didn't tell the police, but she couldn't keep it a secret, so she decided to give you a clue so you'd figure it out, instead. But obviously he decided to silence her."

I frowned. "But I didn't think you even knew anyone in this town, so why did she talk to you?"

Bree looked over her shoulder again. She whispered something angrily, and her shoulders sagged with defeat. She leaned back in her chair and drained her glass in one gulp. "Okay, so, I've never ever told anyone else this before, so it's scary for me. James tells me I can trust you. But..." she sucked in a deep breath. "Okay, here goes. Zen was going to tell you, obviously, before someone shut her up permanently. So she told me, but not while she was alive. I see ghosts."

"Ghosts?"

Of all the things I expected Bree to say – and I did have a vivid imagination – I never anticipated *ghosts*. Were ghosts even real?

Of course they're not real. I just didn't hear right, did I? I must be soooooo drunk.

Bree's voice trembled. She reached for the bottle. "I know, it sounds mad. But it's true. I've seen them all my life. They're drawn to me because they're lonely and I'm the only person who will listen to them. They're really fucking annoying. *Especially* the six in this room right now."

I peered all around the room, half expecting Morrie to jump out from the corner with a sheet over his head. "There are ghosts here?"

"Yes, but don't panic. I brought three of the bastards with me." She glanced over her shoulder again. "The others are your resident spirits. A stooped old man in a monk's habit, a little girl with a stuffed rabbit, and a stern-faced woman wearing a black corset I'd die for, and carrying a stack of occult books. They're quite harmless, and they're very happy with the current caretakers of the shop."

A woman in a black corset with occult books. That sounds like Victoria Bainbridge, the bookseller who owned the shop during the early 1800s.

But Bree couldn't possibly know what Victoria looked like.

It's a coincidence.

Or...she really does see ghosts.

"If you can see ghosts," I say. "Why couldn't you just ask Rasmussen who killed him? Why give us the most cryptic clue in the universe?"

"It doesn't work like that. Not every dead person comes back as a ghost, and those that do cannot remember their own death. It's kind of like waking up in the morning and trying to remember a dream – only random bits come back to you, and they often don't make sense. Zen remembered she had something important to tell you, but all she could recall of the message was the lily. The rest I put together."

"And did she tell you to come to me, instead of the police?"

"The police wouldn't have believed me. But that's not the only reason. The thing is," Bree continued in a rush, "I've had a recent brush with murder myself. And I heard all about you from the village gossip – the bookshop girl in Argleton with the three strange boyfriends who solves crimes the police can't – and I thought, I have to meet this girl. I thought maybe you were like me. And so I maaaaay have stalked you a little."

"You stalked me?" I knew I should be creeped out, but being stalked by Bree was actually flattering.

"Yeah, I mean… It wasn't a serial-killer stalk, I swear. I follow the bookshop Facebook page and I found all the articles in the Argleton Gazette, and I noticed things that didn't make sense. Like the fact that all your boyfriends are named after fictional characters. And the raven that shows up in every story. And someone digging up graves, and the Dracula killer, and the latest suspect disappearing from police custody in a puff of smoke. And I thought, maybe she's like me. But I can see from your face that you think I'm mad, so I'll let myself out—"

She stood to leave.

"No, please don't." I flung out my arm. Big mistake. My entire body lurched, and I slid out of the chair. *So graceful. So drunk.* "Bree, stay. Please. I want to…hic…hear about the ghosts. I may not be like you, but I definitely have my share of…hic…strangeness in my life."

"Oh yeah?"

"Yeah. Like the fact that one of my boyfriends randomly turns into a raven. Or that I'm the daughter of Homer the time-traveling Greek poet. Or…or…a million other things I can't think of right now because I am sooooooo smashed."

Warm hands wrapped around me, helping me to my feet. "Here we go," Bree said. "I think we'd better get you to bed."

"Thanks, friend," I murmured as Bree dragged me to the bedroom. "If you ever find yourself with another murder falling into your lap, you can come here and I'll put my crack team onto it."

She laughed softly as she dropped me onto a heap of masculine limbs. "I appreciate that, Mina. I'm hoping we can hang out a bit even when we don't have a murder to solve…"

She said something else, but my drunken mind couldn't parse it. Heathcliff grunted and threw a heavy arm over me, pulling me into the cuddle pile. In a moment, I was dead to the world.

CHAPTER THIRTY-TWO

"Can I open my eyes yet?" Quoth asked as he gripped Oscar's harness and stepped gingerly onto Butcher Street. I looped my arm in his, and felt his fingers tremble against my skin. As a bird, Quoth relied on his eyesight even more than humans did, and being in total darkness made him nervous.

He had no reason to be nervous, though. We had only good things in store for him.

"This is a weird turn of fate." I pressed my lips to his cheek as I helped him down the steps. "The blind leading the blind."

"Patience, little birdie. All will be revealed." Morrie flung open the door to Ms. Ellis' old house, and Oscar and I helped Quoth navigate the threshold. Heathcliff closed the door behind us and flicked on the lights, and Morrie whipped the blindfold from his eyes. "Voila!"

Quoth's eyes widened as he took in the transformed interior of Mrs. Ellis' old flat. The large sitting room to the left had been converted into a gallery space, with crisp white walls and industrial lighting. The dining room had become a studio and class space with easels and long tables for group projects. The old pink kitchen had been gutted and replaced with deep sinks and a fridge for storing paints, and the walls were hung with Quoth's paintings and some upcycled sculptures made by Earl Larson from junk people dumped by the railroad tracks.

"What *is* this place?" Quoth breathed. His fingers circled my wrist.

"It's yours, birdie," Morrie said. "Yours to do with as you please. We set it up like this with the idea of it being a local gallery and art class space, and there are some simple rooms upstairs that would work for artist retreats, but all the furniture and partitions can be moved around if you have something else in mind."

"It's really more of a favor to us. This will keep beatnik types with their weird hair and patchouli scent out of the shop," Heathcliff said with a hint of hopefulness in his voice.

"But I…" Quoth's gaze raised to the ceiling, where I'd painted hundreds of tiny ravens in flight. "I don't know if I could…"

"We'll help you run it when you have your own classes and can't handle being in your human form," I said. "But you've been doing so well at school that I think you'll be fine."

"And it's not all yours," Heathcliff added. "Mina claimed the basement room as extra storage for the shop, and she says she might use the rooms upstairs for her writing, because apparently she can't write while I'm yelling at customers."

Quoth looked at me. This close, I could see the tears sheening his fire-rimmed eyes. I shook my head. "For once, I had very little to do with this. Morrie and Heathcliff came to me with the idea and asked if I thought you'd like it, and I did paint the ravens because neither of them can draw to save themselves, but they did everything else."

"And before you make a face, it's not because we want you out of the shop," Heathcliff grumbled. "It's not *completely* terrible having you around, especially since you crap on Morrie when he's being annoying."

"We just thought that you should have something of your

own," Morrie said. "A project that could grow with you, something that everyone in the village could enjoy. And you express yourself through your art, so we thought maybe you could help others do that, too."

"I can't…" Quoth's voice choked with emotion. "I can't believe you did all this for me."

"Of course we did, birdie." Morrie stepped toward him. There was a brief pause when neither quite knew what the other would do, but then Morrie strode forward and wrapped Quoth in his arms. "We're brothers," he whispered into Quoth's silken hair, kissing the top of his head. "Don't you ever think otherwise."

"You never told me this was going to turn into *Brokeback Mountain*," Heathcliff muttered, but he too stepped forward and drew the two of them into one of his bone-crushing hugs. Quoth peered up at me from between them, and although it looked like Heathcliff had irreversibly compressed his spine, I don't think I'd ever seen him so happy.

"And I think you should talk to someone."

"But there's no therapist who specializes in…"

"…fictional characters. Right." I grinned at Morrie and Heathcliff. "But that's not true."

"Miss Havisham," Heathcliff growled.

"Miss Havisham," Morrie grinned. "After she drove us crazy with all her wedding magazines and getting her veil caught in the doorway, we sent her off to university in London. We all thought she'd study, but that's the thing about fictional characters in the real world – you never know what you're going to do when your story isn't written for you. She fell in love with psychology. She has a thriving practice now, and she's happy to see you pro bono. She'll even take the train here if you have trouble getting into the city. Although it's probably quicker for you to get to her, as the raven flies."

"I…" Quoth pulled out a chair and slumped into it. "I don't know what to…"

"You don't have to do anything, birdie," Morrie said. "Just keep being yourself."

"Nevermore Bookshop wouldn't be the same without you," Heathcliff said gruffly.

"And look at this," Morrie handed Quoth a book. "We passed it around the village and got people to leave you messages."

Quoth turned the pages. His tears splattered on the paper as he read their lovely notes. Jo had even drawn a beautiful picture of a raven on the inside cover.

"You are *so* wanted." I wrapped my arms around Quoth and squeezed him tight. "Not just by us, but by the whole village. You may have spent most of your life wanting to be invisible, but look at all these lives you've touched. You made a terrible mistake with Dracula, but that doesn't mean that *you* are terrible. That's not who you are inside, you got it?"

Quoth turned to me, his lips brushing mine in an achingly tender kiss. He raised a perfect eyebrow. "I heard that there were bedrooms upstairs?"

"I thought you'd never ask, birdie." Morrie scooped Quoth into his arms and raced for the stairs. Quoth pretended to protest, but when he looked back over his shoulder and saw Heathcliff carrying me behind him, his words died away.

Morrie threw open the door at the end of the hall and barged into the master bedroom. I didn't like to think about what my teacher and her late husband and various boyfriends got up to in there, but I hoped what we were about to do would make her proud.

Morrie dropped Quoth on the bed and flopped down beside him. Quoth's head lolled back and his body jolted when he saw something on the ceiling. "You…you put the sex swing in here?"

"Sure did," Morrie said. "I figured if the whole artist retreat thing didn't work we could turn it into a bordello…"

Heathcliff set me down and I crawled between them, leaning over to touch Quoth's cheek. He beamed at me. "I don't know if having Morrie as my landlord is the best plan to save my sanity."

Morrie leaned across me and pressed his lips to Quoth's forehead. "Just say the word, birdie," he whispered, his tongue darting out to taste Quoth's skin. "I will rock your world."

Quoth laughed as he pushed Morrie playfully away. "I appreciate it, but Mina is all I need."

"Then I suggest you let her ride you before she gets impatient."

Quoth rolled over onto his back, taking me with him. I straddled him, grinding my hips against him as he lay his sweet, tender kisses on me until I forgot there were two other people in the room.

That was until Morrie's sly fingers snaked between us, sliding under my Octavia's Ruin tee to tweak my nipple. Rough hands grabbed the fabric. Heathcliff growled. I grabbed the t-shirt before he could tear it.

"As hot as you literally tearing my clothes off is, I really like this shirt. Tear Morrie's clothes. He can afford to replace them."

"Got it," Heathcliff snarled. I carefully slid my arms through the sleeves and tossed the shirt across the room in the vague direction of the chair. Behind me, I heard the tear of expensive fabric.

"Stop!" Morrie cried out. "That's *silk—*"

His protests were silenced by Heathcliff's lips on his. *Good. That'll shut him up for a bit.*

Quoth slid his hands down my sides, his touch stoking a nervous, weightless feeling in my stomach. It was a feeling I'd come to understand was part of being in love – a sense of complete fullness and yet also a ravenous hunger. Gin, water, pie, chips and mushy peas…nothing could sate that hunger. Nothing except the touch of three remarkable men.

"They're occupied," Quoth whispered, his voice tight with lust.

"They're occupying each other's brains out," I grinned down at him as I drew his black t-shirt over his head to reveal the smooth, wiry planes of his chest and shoulders, the skin like precious porcelain, the bone and sinew and organs that could shift and change and make him another creature, but still Quoth in his heart.

He reached up, held my face in his hands, and brought me down to kiss me. The kind of kiss that was more than a kiss – it was poetry and souls colliding and stars exploding. It was Quoth, and me, and everything we were to each other.

I was so engrossed in kissing Quoth that I didn't remember removing my jeans or his, but gone they were, leaving us naked and writhing, desperate to crawl into each other's skin.

I couldn't see exactly what Heathcliff and Morrie were doing, but I *felt* them with us, and not just in the way that I felt Heathcliff's rough hand play with my nipple, or Morrie's slim fingers dip between my legs to tease my clit. I was *aware* of all three of my boyfriends, touching me, kissing me. It was the same way Quoth's voice appeared inside my head when he was in his bird form. Our connection simply *was*. Even when Heathcliff fucked Morrie, and Morrie fucked Heathcliff, they fucked me in their minds. Each kiss, each caress, each thrust traveled through them into me.

Speaking of fucking...

I lowered myself onto Quoth's shaft, loving the way he sighed with contentment as he filled me. He felt so good, so right, so perfect, like he was made for me. I wriggled my hips to drive him a little deeper, to make him touch every dark and wanton place inside me.

It was amazing to be with three different men at once, because even if I were completely blind, and I couldn't touch them or smell them, I could tell them apart by the way their cocks felt inside me. When Heathcliff drove into me, he threatened to split me in half with the force of his passion. Morrie was controlled chaos, a tempting dance right on the edge of losing control and letting all his devious proclivities take over. Sometimes they do.

And Quoth…Quoth felt like silk – dark and sensuous, almost liquid. As we moved together, it was impossible to tell where his body stopped and mine began.

He reached up to touch my face, so tender, so full of nervous, weightless fluttering as my hips ground down on him.

"You are so beautiful, you must be a dream within a dream," he said, his voice thick with wonder.

"*You* are," I answered with a smile.

"Neither the angels in Heaven above, nor the demons that God hath reviled," whispered Quoth, touching his forehead to mine. "Could ever dissever my soul from the soul, of the beautiful Wilhelmina Wilde."

"Nice rhyme," I grinned. "You should be a poet."

In response, Quoth thrust deep inside me, tilting his hips at the perfect angle to rub my clit against him, to drive me to the edge and over over over into oblivion. His beautiful words washed over me as I tumbled into weightlessness and surrender.

Later, as I lay in their arms, the warmth of my orgasm a dying ember that wrought its ghost inside my belly, I thought about what a wonderful thing it was to live in our bookshop over the magical spring and to love and be loved by a grumpy gothic antihero, a master criminal, and a sweet bird of woe.

CHAPTER THIRTY-THREE

I emerged from the bedroom a few hours later, Quoth perched on my shoulder, preening his feathers. *That's one happy raven.*

We left Heathcliff and Morrie snoring in bed in an adorable tangle, and went in search of snacks. We installed a small fridge in the workshop area, and I was stoked to discover Morrie stocked it with five kinds of cheeses, pickles, relish, and a box of Oliver's famous red velvet cupcakes. I pulled out things and arranged them on a tray when something caught Quoth's eye.

What's that?

Quoth fluttered across the room and picked a white square off the floor by the front door. He dropped it into my lap. It was an envelope. *Mina, it's addressed to you. The postie must've delivered it to the wrong address.*

"Hmmm, he must've. You know how forgetful Deirdre can be sometimes. I wonder what it—" I slit the envelope open and smoothed the letter down on the table so Quoth could read it to me. He glanced at the first line and started hopping up and down with excitement.

"Croak, croak, crooooooooak!"

"Quoth," I laughed. "Stop it. Tell me what it says."

Mina, you got in!

"I got in where? Oh!" I remembered now. "The Meddleworth House writers' retreat. Are you serious?"

Serious as a gothic poet with no sense of humor. Quoth tugged something else from the envelope – a glossy brochure for Meddleworth House, the gorgeous estate nestled in the north of England. It looked like the perfect place to write and learn and dream.

"I got in." I stared at the glossy pictures of writers talking animatedly in front of a roaring fire and looking pensively across the sweeping gardens. I picked up Quoth and hugged him to my chest. "I can't believe it. I got in!"

"Croooooooak," he warbled.

Mina, I love that you're excited, but I...can't...breathe.

"Oops, sorry." I loosened my grip on Quoth.

"What's all the noise down here?" Heathcliff growled. I glanced over my shoulder and saw the outline of him and Morrie on the stairs. "It sounds like someone let in a bunch of customers."

"I got in!" I yelled, leaping from my seat and running into his arms. "I'm going on the writer's retreat!"

"I knew you could do it," Heathcliff whispered into my hair as he held me in a bone-crushing embrace.

Morrie was already tapping away on his phone. "Hey, this place looks fancy. They have an onsite boutique hotel, and an award-winning restaurant nestled in the extensive gardens. There's even a topiary maze and a folly. And look at this list of pampering treatments for their guests. Maybe we should all go along? *Some* of us could do with a mud pack and a manicure." He held up Heathcliff's hand to inspect his cuticles.

"I'm perfectly fine the way I am." Heathcliff yanked his hand from Morrie's grasp.

"They have one of the most extensive private libraries in the country," Morrie said casually, scrolling on his phone. "And a self-reflection chamber where no one disturbs you for hours."

"Then sign me up," Heathcliff said.

Quoth fluttered over and landed on Morrie's shoulder. He peered down at the phone screen. *Look at the sculpture workshop, and the art gallery. I could get ideas for the Nevermore art center. And there's even an unkindness of ravens living on the property.*

Quoth's fire-rimmed eyes widened at the thought of hanging out with some of his kind.

"It's settled," I said. "We're all going to Meddleworth House. Two weeks of spa treatments, writing inspiration, and hanging with ravens."

"And absolutely no murders," said Heathcliff firmly.

"And absolutely no murders," I agreed. "Surely our bad luck can't follow us to this picturesque place?"

TO BE CONTINUED

A poisoned pen drops Mina into a world of trouble when she attends her writer's retreat at Meddleworth House. Luckily she's got Quoth, Morrie, and Heathcliff on hand to solve the case in the next Nevermore Bookshop mystery, Crime and Publishing.

http://books2read.com/crimeandpublishing

Did you love Bree and her ghostly love life? Bree's getting her own series – The Grimdale Graveyard Mysteries – and Mina, Heathcliff, Morrie, Quoth, and other characters will make regular appearances.

To stay up-to-date on when this new paranormal reverse harem releases, AND to get a bonus scene from Quoth's POV and Heathcliff's shop rules, sign up to the Steffanie Holmes newsletter.

http://www.steffanieholmes.com/newsletter

FROM THE AUTHOR

Welcome back to Nevermore Bookshop. I know it's been a while since we stepped through the front door to meet a grumpy, loveable giant, a suave and cheeky criminal genius, and a beautiful and kind raven – and let us not forget the stuffed armadillo.

I had a lot of fun writing this book, especially hunting out Shakespearean insults and reminiscing about my days of amateur theatre. The first play I ever performed in was *A Midsomer Night's Dream* – I was nameless fairy number four – and I've been everyone from one of the Weird Sisters to Falstaff to Queen Elizabeth in *Richard III*.

There's something magical about the theatre, and especially about the way Shakespeare's plays transport us to another time and place while also reminding us how utterly human we all are.

The New New Globe is inspired by the Pop-Up Globe, a project launched right here in New Zealand where a replica of Shakespeare's Globe Theatre made of scaffolding "popped-up" in different places across the city. I was lucky to attend several shows at this unique venue, which had grand plans to travel around the world before the pandemic gave the Pop-Up Globe its final curtain call.

There are two more books to go in the Nevermore Bookshop Mysteries, and if you enjoyed reading about Bree and her ghostly boyfriends, you'll be happy to know she's getting her own series. The Grimdale Graveyard Mysteries will feature regular visits from Mina, Heathcliff, Morrie, Quoth, Jo, and the rest of the gang. The best way to stay up-to-date with when this series releases is by signing up for my newsletter: http://steffanieholmes.com/newsletter.

A portion of the proceeds from every Nevermore book sold go toward supporting Blind Low Vision NZ Guide Dogs, and I'm always sharing cute guide dog pictures and vids in my newsletter.

I wanted to say a huge shout out to contest winner Jeannette Tiburcio, who got to name a victim in this book. She chose the name Zenzile Monroe, based off a childhood friend. The name Zenzile means "you're responsible for what you become," which I absolutely love!

I'm so happy you enjoyed this story! I'd love it if you wanted to leave a review on Amazon or Goodreads. It will help other readers to find their next read.

Thank you, thank you! I love you heaps! Until next time.

Steffanie

ENJOY THIS EXCERPT FROM MY STOLEN LIFE

PROLOGUE: MACKENZIE

I roll over in bed and slam against a wall.

Huh? Odd.

My bed isn't pushed against a wall. I must've twisted around in my sleep and hit the headboard. I do thrash around a lot, especially when I have bad dreams, and tonights was particularly gruesome. My mind stretches into the silence, searching for the tendrils of my nightmare. *I'm lying in bed and some dark shadow comes and lifts me up, pinning my arms so they hurt. He drags me downstairs to my mother, slumped in her favorite chair. At first, I think she passed out drunk after a night at the club, but then I see the dark pool expanding around her feet, staining the designer rug.*

I see the knife handle sticking out of her neck.

I see her glassy eyes rolled toward the ceiling.

I see the window behind her head, and my own reflection in the glass, my face streaked with blood, my eyes dark voids of pain and hatred.

But it's okay now. It was just a dream. It's—

OW.

I hit the headboard again. I reach down to rub my elbow, and my hand grazes a solid wall of satin. On my other side.

What the hell?

I open my eyes into a darkness that is oppressive and complete, the kind of darkness I'd never see inside my princess bedroom with its flimsy purple curtains letting in the glittering skyline of the city. The kind of darkness that folds in on me, pressing me against the hard, un-bedlike surface I lie on.

Now the panic hits.

I throw out my arms, kick with my legs. I hit walls. Walls all around me, lined with satin, dense with an immense weight pressing from all sides. Walls so close I can't sit up or bend my knees. I scream, and my scream bounces back at me, hollow and weak.

I'm in a coffin. I'm in a motherfucking coffin, and I'm *still alive.*

I scream and scream and scream. The sound fills my head and stabs at my brain. I know all I'm doing is using up my precious oxygen, but I can't make myself stop. In that scream I lose myself, and every memory of who I am dissolves into a puddle of terror.

When I do stop, finally, I gasp and pant, and I taste blood and stale air on my tongue. A cold fear seeps into my bones. Am I dying? My throat crawls with invisible bugs. Is this what it feels like to die?

I hunt around in my pockets, but I'm wearing purple pajamas, and the only thing inside is a bookmark Daddy gave me. I can't see it of course, but I know it has a quote from Julius Caesar on it. *Alea iacta est. The die is cast.*

Like fuck it is.

I think of Daddy, of everything he taught me – memories too dark to be obliterated by fear. Bile rises in my throat. I swallow, choke it back. Daddy always told me our world is forged in blood. I might be only thirteen, but I know who he is, what he's capable of. I've heard the whispers. I've seen the way people hurry to appease him whenever he enters a room. I've had the lessons from Antony in what to do if I find myself alone with one of Daddy's enemies.

Of course, they never taught me what to do if one of those enemies *buries me alive.*

I can't give up.

I claw at the satin on the lid. It tears under my fingers, and I pull out puffs of stuffing to reach the wood beneath. I claw at the surface, digging splinters under my nails. Cramps arc along my arm from the awkward angle. I know it's hopeless; I know I'll never be able to scratch my way through the wood. Even if I can, I *feel* the weight of several feet of dirt above me. I'd be crushed in moments. But I have to try.

I'm my father's daughter, and this is not how I die.

I claw and scratch and tear. I lose track of how much time passes in the tiny space. My ears buzz. My skin weeps with cold sweat.

A noise reaches my ears. A faint shifting. A scuffle. A scrape and thud above my head. Muffled and far away.

Someone piling the dirt in my grave.

Or maybe…

…maybe someone digging it out again.

Fuck, fuck, please.

"Help." My throat is hoarse from screaming. I bang the lid with my fists, not even feeling the splinters piercing my skin. "Help me!"

THUD. Something hits the lid. The coffin groans. My veins burn with fear and hope and terror.

The wood cracks. The lid is flung away. Dirt rains down on me, but I don't care. I suck in lungfuls of fresh, crisp air. A circle of light blinds me. I fling my body up, up into the unknown. Warm arms catch me, hold me close.

"I found you, Claws." Only Antony calls me by that nickname. Of course, it would be my cousin who saves me. Antony drags me over the lip of the grave, *my* grave, and we fall into crackling leaves and damp grass.

I sob into his shoulder. Antony rolls me over, his fingers pressing all over my body, checking if I'm hurt. He rests my back against cold stone. "I have to take care of this," he says. I watch through tear-filled eyes as he pushes the dirt back into the hole – into what was supposed to be my grave – and brushes dead leaves on top. When he's done, it's impossible to tell the ground's been disturbed at all.

I tremble all over. I can't make myself stop shaking. Antony comes back to me and wraps me in his arms. He staggers to his feet, holding me like I'm weightless. He's only just turned eighteen, but already he's built like a tank.

I let out a terrified sob. Antony glances over his shoulder, and there's panic in his eyes. "You've got to be quiet, Claws," he whispers. "They might be nearby. I'm going to get you out of here."

I can't speak. My voice is gone, left in the coffin with my screams. Antony hoists me up and darts into the shadows. He runs with ease, ducking between rows of crumbling gravestones and beneath bent and gnarled trees. Dimly, I recognize this place – the old Emerald Beach cemetery, on the edge of Beaumont Hills overlooking the bay, where the original families of Emerald Beach buried their dead.

Where someone tried to bury me.

Antony bursts from the trees onto a narrow road. His car is parked in the shadows. He opens the passenger door and settles me inside before diving behind the wheel and gunning the engine.

We tear off down the road. Antony rips around the deadly corners like he's on a racetrack. Steep cliffs and crumbling old mansions pass by in a blur.

"My parents…" I gasp out. "Where are my parents?"

"I'm sorry, Claws. I didn't get to them in time. I only found you."

I wait for this to sink in, for the fact I'm now an orphan to hit me in a rush of grief. But I'm numb. My body won't stop shaking, and I left my brain and my heart buried in the silence of that coffin.

"Who?" I ask, and I fancy I catch a hint of my dad's cold savagery in my voice. "Who did this?"

"I don't know yet, but if I had to guess, it was Brutus. I warned your dad that he was making alliances and building up to a challenge. I think he's just made his move."

I try to digest this information. Brutus – who was once my father's trusted friend, who'd eaten dinner at our house and played Chutes and Ladders with me – killed my parents and buried me alive. But it bounces off the edge of my skull and doesn't stick. The life I had before, my old life, it's gone, and as I twist and grasp for memories, all I grab is stale coffin air.

"What now?" I ask.

Antony tosses his phone into my lap. "Look at the headlines."

I read the news app he's got open, but the words and images blur together. "This… this doesn't make any sense…"

"They think you're dead, Claws," Antony says. "That means you have to *stay* dead until we're strong enough to move against him. Until then, you have to be a ghost. But don't worry, I'll protect you. I've got a plan. We'll hide you where they'll never think to look."

Start reading:
http://books2read.com/mystolenlife

MORE FROM THE AUTHOR OF SHUNNED

From the author of *Shunned*, the Amazon top-20 bestselling bully romance readers are calling, "The greatest mindf**k of 2019," comes this new dark contemporary high school reverse harem romance.

Psst. I have a secret.

Are you ready?

I'm Mackenzie Malloy, and everyone thinks they know who I am.

Five years ago, I disappeared.

No one has seen me or my family outside the walls of Malloy Manor since.
But now I'm coming to reclaim my throne:
The Ice Queen of Stonehurst Prep is back.

Standing between me and my everything?
Three things can bring me down:

The sweet guy who wants answers from his former friend.
The rock god who wants to f*ck me.
The king who'll crush me before giving up his crown.

They think they can ruin me, wreck it all, but I won't let them.
I'm not the Mackenzie Eli used to know.
Hot boys and rock gods like Gabriel won't win me over.
And just like Noah, I'll kill to keep my crown.

I'm just a poor little rich girl with the stolen life.
I'm here to tear down three princes,
before they destroy me.

Read now:
http://books2read.com/mystolenlife

OTHER BOOKS BY STEFFANIE HOLMES

Nevermore Bookshop Mysteries

A Dead and Stormy Night

Of Mice and Murder

Pride and Premeditation

How Heathcliff Stole Christmas

Memoirs of a Garroter

Prose and Cons

A Novel Way to Die

Much Ado About Murder

Crime and Publishing

Plot and Bothered

Kings of Miskatonic Prep

Shunned

Initiated

Possessed

Ignited

Stonehurst Prep

My Stolen Life

My Secret Heart

My Broken Crown

My Savage Kingdom

DARK ACADEMIA

Pretty Girls Make Graves

Brutal Boys Cry Blood

Manderley Academy

Ghosted

Haunted

Spirited

Briarwood Witches

Earth and Embers

Fire and Fable

Water and Woe

Wind and Whispers

Spirit and Sorrow

Crookshollow Gothic Romance

Art of Cunning (Alex & Ryan)

Art of the Hunt (Alex & Ryan)

Art of Temptation (Alex & Ryan)

The Man in Black (Elinor & Eric)

Watcher (Belinda & Cole)

Reaper (Belinda & Cole)

Wolves of Crookshollow

Digging the Wolf (Anna & Luke)

Writing the Wolf (Rosa & Caleb)

Inking the Wolf (Bianca & Robbie)

Wedding the Wolf (Willow & Irvine)

ABOUT THE AUTHOR

Steffanie Holmes is the *USA Today* bestselling author of the paranormal, gothic, dark, and fantastical. Her books feature clever, witty heroines, secret societies, creepy old mansions and alpha males who *always* get what they want.

Legally-blind since birth, Steffanie received the 2017 Attitude Award for Artistic Achievement. She was also a finalist for a 2018 Women of Influence award.

Steff is the creator of *Rage Against the Manuscript* – a resource of free content, books, and courses to help writers tell their story, find their readers, and build a badass writing career.

Steffanie lives in New Zealand with her husband, a horde of cantankerous cats, and their medieval sword collection.

STEFFANIE HOLMES NEWSLETTER

Grab a free copy of *Cabinet of Curiosities* – a Steffanie Holmes compendium of short stories and bonus scenes – when you sign up for updates with the Steffanie Holmes newsletter.

http://www.steffanieholmes.com/newsletter

Come hang with Steffanie
www.steffanieholmes.com
steff@steffanieholmes.com

♪

Printed in Great Britain
by Amazon